The Deadly Art of Love and Murder

A Caribou King Mystery

by

Linda Crowder

For information, email **Cozy Cat Press**, cozycatpress@aol.com or visit our website at: www.cozycatpress.com

COZY CAT
P R E S S

ISBN: 978-1-946063-37-3

Printed in the United States of America

Cover design by Paula Ellenberger
www.paulaellenberger.com

1 2 3 4 5 6 7 8 9 10

To my mom, Lucy Miller, without whom I would never have written a word.

Chapter 1

If I'd known I was going to find a dead body, I would have stayed in bed. It had been the most successful season ever for my fine arts gallery in Coho Bay, Alaska, but the last week had been insane. By the time the final ship sailed, I had been ready to sleep for a month. When I get tired, I get sick and since I never do anything half-way, for three weeks the world went by without me. That's why I was late checking on the Tilamu house. Not that anything would have been different had I been there on time, but I like to think I could have done something to save her.

It had started snowing on the last day of the season and it hadn't stopped. One storm after another pounded our tiny town. That's not unusual in January, but since it was only October, the weather had been the talk of the town. For the longest month of my life, I'd been holed up in my apartment with my mother, who was in full Florence Nightingale mode. I love her, but when the sun finally peeped out from the clouds, I didn't hesitate to make a break for it.

Plodding along the boardwalk, my movement was hampered by the snowmobile pants I was wearing over the top of my jeans, which were over the top of a pair of long underwear. They had been my mother's suggestion and she'd refused to budge until I agreed to put them on. She thought I was crazy to tromp all the way out here. "Your father will have turned off the water, Caribou, and if he didn't, there's no rush."

She was right, of course. If the pipes were frozen, they weren't likely to thaw until spring but that was entirely beside the point. "I called him, but he must be out of range. It's gonna bug me if I don't go."

We both knew I just wanted an excuse to get out, but she must have been feeling as cooped up as I had because she'd given up the argument after I'd agreed to the long underwear. When I'd emerged from the bedroom, she'd been standing by the door, her overnight bag packed and ready to go. I'd kissed her cheek and we went our separate ways, her to my sister's apartment and me to check on the Tilamu house.

I didn't relish calling Anne Buchanan. Along with her siblings, she had inherited the house when their father died and she hated spending money. I'd likely get another earful from her, blaming the crumbling of the cottage on my shoddy management. Maybe I'd try to reach Alex instead. He wouldn't want to fix the pipes either, but at least he wouldn't yell at me. His other sister, Agatha Kirby, hadn't spoken to me in years so she'd be no help.

Plumbing wasn't the only problem with the house. It needed a new furnace, a roof, added insulation, paint and could benefit from updating in the kitchen and bath. I wouldn't have been able to rent it at all if Mrs. Nash hadn't insisted on staying there every year. She was in her eighties and hadn't aged much more gracefully than the house, but she had a strong sentimental attachment to it. I hated the thought of putting her into such a dilapidated shack, but she wouldn't budge.

There were sixteen houses huddled between the forest on one side and the bay on the other. Doc Tilamu had served as a medic in the Navy, then had gone to medical school on the GI Bill. He'd brought his newly-minted license home to Alaska, building the house for his bride, with whom he spent the next fifty-four years.

They'd had three children who moved away the minute they'd been old enough to go. As far as I knew, they'd never returned. They didn't even visit, though Doc and his wife used to go south to visit them until his wife died. The house didn't earn them much in rent and I often wondered why they bothered to hang onto it, but it wasn't my place to tell them to sell.

I arrived at the door feeling like an icicle and stomped my feet in the entryway, hoping to pound feeling back into them. It wasn't much warmer inside than out and I grimaced to think how cold it must be under the house. I kept my coat on and walked into the kitchen, expecting to find the keys on the counter and a note from Mrs. Nash. What I didn't expect to find was the woman herself, but there she was, slumped sideways on the couch, half covered in snow. My mouth had already opened to say hello when my brain finished processing what I was seeing. Her skin was white and her face was... missing. The broken window beside her had let in three weeks of snow, effectively turning the room into a deep freeze.

I'm not normally a screamer, but looking at what was left of that sweet old woman, drew a sound from my throat that I hadn't known I was capable of making. Mom would have said it was a sound that would wake the dead, but it didn't have any effect on Mrs. Nash. That was a blessing because, I didn't relish being on the forefront of the zombie apocalypse. After my session of primal screaming, I finally persuaded my legs to move and did what any self-respecting, modern woman would do. I got the heck out of there.

What happened next is a bit of a blur, but I might have screamed all the way from the Tilamu house to City Hall. What I do remember is that when I burst through the door, Coho Bay's part-time receptionist and full-time match maker, Tammy Atumwa, threw the stack of papers she'd been holding into the air and started screaming along with me. Of course, she had no idea why I was screaming but Tammy was never one to let that keep her from enjoying a good show.

Dan Simmons, our one-man police force, ran in from his office, gun drawn. When he saw me, he holstered his gun and grabbed my arms. "Cara, what is it?"

I put my hands over my mouth, forcing myself to be still but I could still hear somebody screaming. I hoped it wasn't me, but I wasn't sure until Dan shouted at Tammy, "For the love of Pete, cut it out!"

The silence was deafening and I started to shake. Dan tightened his grip. "What's wrong? You look like you've seen a ghost."

An image of the faceless Mrs. Nash rising up and floating across the room flashed through my head and by the time I got control of myself again, I noticed I'd drawn a crowd. Two part-time city employees, the mayor and a councilman were watching us from the hallway. Their excited expressions suggested they'd seen too much reality television and couldn't tell the difference between genuine trauma and entertainment.

Dan's voice was calm and reassuring, cutting through my confusion and dismay at being the unwanted center of attention. "What's wrong, Cara?"

I took a deep breath, then told him about finding Mrs. Nash's body. I forced myself to tell him about her face and the snow and the spatters of blood all over the wall. Instead of doing whatever it is a policeman should do when someone is telling him a story like this, Dan simply stared at me. The lines on his forehead deepened and his head tilted to one side. He never took his eyes off me, but when I finished talking, he told Tammy to call my father.

"Why do you want Dad?" I asked as she picked up the phone.

The lines vanished as the muscles in his face relaxed. "That's the first thing you've said that made sense."

"What do you mean? I told you everything, Dan."

"You've been talking, Cara. I don't know what you've been saying, but it sure wasn't English."

I looked at Tammy, who nodded as she spoke into the phone. I turned to the crowd and the men mumbled and nodded, shuffling their feet and consulting with each other in hushed tones. I grabbed Dan's arm, concentrating hard, making each word come out distinctly, almost as a separate sentence. "Mrs. Nash. Dead. Frozen."

"Frozen? Where?"

I frowned, not understanding. "She's frozen to death, Dan. Only she must've been dead before she froze, because her face is gone."

There was more shuffling from the men in the hallway and Dan rubbed the back of his neck with the hand I wasn't gripping. "I meant where is she, Cara."

"That makes so much more sense. She's at the Tilamu house. I went to turn the water off and I found her."

"The Kings are on their way." Tammy sounded remarkably calm and I felt a flash of resentment that she could turn her emotions on and off so quickly.

"Dan, I'm fine," I said, trying to straighten my back, but wobbling a bit too much to pull it off.

"That's why your face is gray and you're shaking so hard I can hardly hold you up. Why don't you sit down?"

I started to shake my head, but it turned into a nod somewhere in the middle. "Maybe I should sit." Once the idea came into my head, my knees took care of the rest.

Dan crouched down next to me on the floor. "I was thinking about the couch, but suit yourself."

I tried to glare at him but my face wasn't following directions and it came out feeling more wild-eyed than withering. "I just need to catch my breath." I grasped my knees and ducked my head, wondering whether I was going to throw up now or if I could hold out until later.

"What are you doing to my daughter, Daniel? Why is she on the floor?" Bless her heart, my mother must have run all the way from my sister's apartment. She pushed Dan away, depositing him unceremoniously on his rear end and put her hand on my back. "Caribou, are you ill again? I knew you were trying to do too much too soon."

"Mom, I'm okay." Since I wasn't able to lift my head, I didn't think she believed me.

My father, who'd been right behind her, pulled me into his lap like he used to do when I was five years old and would crash my bike on the gravel roads. I threw my arms around him and dissolved into sobs that shook my whole body. "Daddy, she's dead. She's dead and her face is gone! It's horrible."

Mom scrambled to her feet, like a she-bear protecting her cub. "What is Caribou talking about, Daniel? Who's dead?" Not giving him time to answer, she wheeled on the assemblage. "Why are you all standing there like a pack of jackals?"

Feet shuffled backward, leaving the mayor to face her alone. "Cara came in like this, Marcie. Dan's been trying to calm her down."

"She's freaked about something, that's for sure," observed Bent Andrews, my brother-in-law. He must have followed my parents at a more sedate pace, making sure my sister Mel didn't slip on the icy boardwalk.

"She says she found Mrs. Nash frozen to death at the Tilamu house," explained Dan.

"No, not that, Dan." I was still sitting on Dad's lap, fighting to get control of myself.

"You told me she was frozen," said Dan.

"She's frozen, but her face…" I buried mine in my father's shoulder. That image was going to be with me for a lifetime.

"Is gone. I forgot."

"How can you forget a thing like that?" My mother might have kicked him if there hadn't been witnesses. Dan must have thought so too, because he scrambled to his feet and put a little distance between them.

"That's horrible," gasped Mel. "Cara, are you sure?"

"The way she's been screaming," said the mayor, "I think the whole town's sure by now."

"Don't you make fun of her, Clemson Solokov! I suppose it wouldn't bother you to have found some poor woman's face blown off, but my daughter has feelings." The mayor looked around, finally noticing the other men had retreated, then took a few steps back to join them. Mom turned her attention Dan. "Why are you just standing there? A woman's been murdered. Do something about it!"

"Nobody said she was murdered, Marcie." Dan didn't sound intimidated, but he did take a step back, bumping into a potted fichus tree. "It was probably suicide."

"We ought to take a look, Dan," suggested Bent.

"Not me," said Mel, shuddering and running a hand over her belly.

Bent put his arm around her. "I wasn't talkin' about you, honey."

"Why are you so quick to call it a suicide, Daniel?" asked my mother. "Are you trying to cover up for someone or are you too lazy to do the job we pay you for?"

My father helped me to my feet. Once he saw I could stand, he put a hand on Mom's shoulder. I heard sighs and mumbling from the city staff and I wondered about my mother's reputation. "Calm down, Marcie. Cara's all right. I'm sure Dan will consider every possibility in his investigation."

"Don't you patronize me, Robert King." Mom stabbed a finger into his chest, but she did stop threatening people.

Dan stepped away from the fichus and strode to the reception counter. "Tammy, call the state and have them send out the suspicious death team. I'll head over to the Tilamu house and see what we've got."

Solokov cleared his throat. "Dan, there's no need to bring in the state if it's a suicide." He turned to the city councilman for agreement, but the man had fled deeper into the hallway at the look my mother threw the mayor.

"Who are you covering up for, Clemson?" asked my mother and Solokov winced.

"Mrs. Nash was a sweet lady," said Mel. "She wouldn't have killed herself."

"She had a smile on her face every time I saw her," Tammy added, eager to contribute to the conversation. Dan glared at her and she picked up the phone.

Solokov stopped her. "Just a minute, Tammy. Dan, the state will bill us for coming out here. The city can't afford to incur that cost if her death was just a suicide."

"Just a suicide," said my mother, shaking her head. "You are a sorry excuse for a human being."

At this, the mayor appeared to discover his spine. "You take that back, Marcie. I'm acting in the best interest of the people."

"Mrs. Nash was one of those people."

"She was not a resident of this town."

"What difference does that make?" asked my dad. "Stop pinching pennies, Clem. I'm all for fiscal responsibility, but we owe it to Mrs. Nash to take a scientific approach to this."

The mayor bristled. "I don't need advice from a tree hugger. If it were up to you two, we'd have spent the cruise ship revenue twelve times over."

My father's eyes narrowed. "I am an environmental scientist."

The two men stood toe to toe for a few minutes, each taking the measure of the other, then Solokov backed away. "You can't tell what's going on inside another person's head. She was what, a hundred years old?"

"Eighty-one," I said, "and for what it's worth, I don't think she killed herself either."

"Well just pull out your checkbook then, missy. We'll have the state send you the bill."

Dan pulled his coat from a hook by the door. "I'm going to go do my job." He looked pointedly at my mother. "Tammy, make that call or I will."

Tammy's hand hovered over the phone. Dan, as the city's only full-time employee, was effectively her boss but Solokov signed her checks. She looked from one man to the other, then out at my parents and finally at me, but I didn't know what to tell her. "I can take you over there," I offered, deflecting attention from Tammy, who shot me a grateful look and picked up the phone. I hoped Dan would turn me down because the last thing in the world I wanted to do was go back to the Tilamu house.

Mom came to my rescue. "Caribou, you are not putting yourself through that again." She laid her hand on my arm and looked at Dan, her voice firm. "He doesn't need you."

"I'll go," offered Bent.

"You stay with Mel," said Dad. "I'll go."

"None of you are going." We turned to stare at Dan. "I'll take a look first, Clem, but if there's any doubt in my mind that Mrs. Nash killed herself, I'm calling the state."

"That's all I've been asking," Solokov answered.

Dan looked at me and his expression softened. "I'll stop by when I can and let you know when you can have the house back."

"The pipes," I said, remembering why I'd gone there in the first place. "Dad, did you shut off the water at the end of the season?"

"Oh shoot, honey. I'm sorry. I didn't even think about it."

"Will you check the shut-off while you're there Dan?"

He smiled, "There's my girl, feet back in the real world." He ducked out, leaving my mother to glare at his retreating back.

***

"She was the sweetest thing." Mel put a steaming mug of cocoa on the table in front of me. "I can't believe she'd kill herself."

Mom nodded, stirring her tea. "She always had a kind word when you'd see her on the street."

"Did it look like she killed herself, Cara?" Dad asked.

I shuddered, not wanting to think about how Mrs. Nash had looked. "I don't know. I wasn't thinking too clearly." I took a drink of cocoa, letting its warmth flow through me. "Mmmmmm, this is really good, Mel."

"Vanilla vodka." She took a sip from her own mug, which was plain chocolate. "I thought you could use a little something."

"It's heavenly. Pity you can't have any." Mel smiled and her hand went to her midsection. Bent leaned over, kissing the top of her head as she blushed.

"You said she was frozen?" asked my father, pulling my attention back to Mrs. Nash.

"The window was broken." Away from that house, surrounded by my family, it was getting easier to talk about it. "She was half buried in snow."

"Thank goodness for small favors." Mom shuddered. "Otherwise, it would have been a horrible scene."

"It was plenty grizzly as it was, thank you very much."

"The snow started at the end of the season," said Mel. "Maybe she'd assumed you'd find her right away."

"She may have been dead longer," said Bent. "Anybody remember the last time you saw her?"

The phone rang before we could answer and he went to pick it up. I devoted myself to my cocoa while the others talked. Mom and Dad were going to convert the unfinished space upstairs to a guest room, second bath and family room. They planned to stay until Mel's baby was born, then help out in the first few months, when sleep can be a precious commodity for new parents.

Mel and Bent weren't too thrilled, but they told themselves it was only temporary. Our parents loved their log house, even if it was five miles out of town and they hoped once spring came, they'd be helping them move back out there. I couldn't picture my mother being content to be so far away from her first grandchild, but I'd stopped teasing Mel about them building on the vacant lot they owned next door to her restaurant. I don't want to bite the hand that feeds me and Bent is a wicked good cook.

"Jack thinks he and Frank can finish our order by the end of next week," Dad was explaining to Mel. "He had some lumber on hand so we took what would fit in the truck. Frank'll deliver the rest when he gets through for the day."

Frank Baker had moved to Coho Bay from Seattle last year to pilot a tour boat for cruisers, but he'd bonded with Jack Lennon and had started working at the mill with him when the season ended. Frank was good looking, tall and confident about his appeal to women. He'd flirted with me a bit during the season and I'd mostly blown him off. By the time I realized he was genuinely interested, I'd been too sick to care. Mom told me he'd stopped by several times while I'd been sick but after taking one look in the mirror, I'd threatened to kill her if she let him see me. I'm already unusually tall, rail thin and have flaming red hair. Add in puffy eyes, runny nose and the aroma of mentholated ointment and any hope of romance would fly right out the window.

Bent came back into the dining room, interrupting my thoughts. "That was Dan."

"Was it a suicide?" I asked.

"He's not sure, little sister." He walked over to where our coats hung by the door and shrugged into his. "He'll give you the details when he gets here. He wants to talk to you. I'm going to go secure the house for him until the state gets here."

Mom and Mel fell into a discussion about baby names and Dad went to finish unloading lumber. I should have offered to help, but I sat staring into my mug, trying to remember the last time I'd spoken with Mrs. Nash. I closed my eyes and pictured her, not as I'd just seen her, but as I'd always known her. She'd been a pixie of a woman, with wrinkled cheeks and wispy white hair who always smelled of vanilla and arthritis cream. She wore cotton blouses over polyester pants and always carried a brown purse over one arm. No matter how warm it was, she'd worn a yellow sweater she'd knitted herself.

She'd been funny and showed an interest in everyone and everything. There might have been a whiff of loneliness about her, but she never seemed sad or depressed. It was hard to imagine her taking her own life, especially in such a brutal way. Still, Mayor Solokov was right. You don't know what's going on inside someone. I doubted she would have opened up to me if she'd been struggling with depression because in spite of the years I'd known her, we hadn't had that kind of relationship. I suddenly felt very tired.

The bells on the door jingled and I looked up to see Dan stomping the snow from his boots. His expression was grim and it didn't lighten when my sister brought him a slice of apple pie. He nodded his thanks and sat down in the chair across from me. My mother rose to get him coffee and he thanked her, harsh words forgotten. In a small town, it doesn't pay to hold grudges.

"Bentley told us you think Mrs. Nash might have been murdered." Thank goodness my mother could speak because a lump had risen in my throat and I was having trouble breathing.

"Possibly."

"Did you find a note?"

"Lots of suicides don't leave notes." He grunted as he forked another piece of pie.

Mom sat down next to me. "Daniel, are we going to have to drag it out of you word by word?"

He put down his fork. "Would it do me any good to tell you I can't talk about an open investigation?"

"No, it would not. Caribou is going to be seeing Mrs. Nash's body every time she closes her eyes, possibly for the rest of her life. Our interest is hardly idle curiosity."

Dan returned to his pie. "It looks like suicide."

"But you aren't sure?" I asked.

"Suicide seems the most likely answer, but I want to be sure. I'm suspicious by nature."

I swirled the dregs of chocolate in my mug. "Why would anyone want to kill such a sweet old lady?"

"I have no idea."

"Burglary?" suggested Mel.

"I didn't see any jewelry, but I don't know what she might have had. There weren't any credit cards in her purse, but she still had two hundred dollars in cash."

"She always paid cash for her meals," Mel explained. "I don't think she approved of credit cards."

"Still, if the killer left the cash behind, Melody, it couldn't have been a robbery."

"Maybe he broke in when she was gone and she came home and caught him rifling the house," I offered, but even I didn't believe it. "Maybe he shot her then got scared and ran away."

"He left the gun behind," said Dan. "Besides, she was sitting on the couch. That's not where I'd be if I'd startled a burglar."

My mother squeezed my hand. "I know we don't want to believe Mrs. Nash would kill herself, Caribou, but the condition of that house would not inspire someone to break in thinking he would find something of value."

"Was the window broken from the outside, Dan?"

"State boys will have to dig the snow out to know that."

"What kind of gun?" I asked, though I had a sinking feeling I knew the answer.

"Snub-nosed .357."

Mel's eyes widened. "That's an awfully big gun for an old woman. It had to be murder, Dan."

"Melody is right, Daniel. I can't picture Mrs. Nash having a gun at all, let alone a monster like that."

"The gun was hers." I felt like putting my head down on the table and crying. "She liked to go for walks. She'd go out early in the morning before the ships got here or later, after the tourists left. She said it kept her young. After Johnny was attacked by that bear, she asked me what she should do."

"And you advised a little old lady to buy a gun?" asked Dan.

I flinched as though he'd slapped me. "I sent her to Bear Tooth to get a can of bear spray. The next time I saw her, she told me she'd bought a gun instead."

"Daniel, with all you've told us, I'm puzzled why you are not satisfied that her death was a suicide. Didn't the wound appear self-inflicted?"

"It's hard to tell with the body being in the condition it's in, Mrs. King."

My mother made a face. "You've been calling me Marcie for years. There's no reason to start 'Mrs. Kinging' me because you've decided you'd like to date my daughter."

"Mother!" I kicked at her under the table. Where on earth had she come up with the idea that Dan wanted to go out with me? I put my head on my hands and willed the floor to open up and swallow me.

Dan went on as if he hadn't heard. "Tell me about Mrs. Nash."

"What do you want to know?" Mel asked.

"Where was she from?"

"Originally Minnesota but she and her husband moved to Arizona after he retired."

"I don't remember her having a husband."

"He's been dead, how long would you say, Mother, twenty years?"

"About that long, yes. He passed the year after Mrs. Tilamu died. That was the first year she rented from us. She and her husband used to stay with the Tilamus but after both her husband and his wife died, she thought tongues would wag so she rented one of our cabins."

"Only Doc was too much of a gentleman to let her stay in a dry cabin so every year, she'd pay the rent, but he'd move out to the cabin and let her have the house," I finished, glad to be talking about anything other than my non-existent love life. "I thought it was sweet."

"Like, how sweet?" asked Dan, one eyebrow raised.

"It's not what you're thinking," said Mel. "Her husband went to med school with Doc. The men went fishing and hunting while their wives hung out together."

"But she kept coming up after both her husband and Doc's wife died. Didn't you think that was strange?"

"Actually, I did," admitted my mother. "I asked her about it. As I remember, she told me that when summer came, she found herself packing up as usual and coming here. She didn't know what else to do with her summer, they'd been coming for so long. Doc was happy to see her, though. I think their mutual grief brought them some measure of comfort."

"How did her husband die?" I asked.

"He was killed in a car accident, I believe."

"I always thought she and Doc would get married."

"They never had that kind of relationship, Caribou. They were friends. That's all."

"What about family?" asked Dan.

"Yes, I suppose you will need to contact her next of kin." Mom tapped her fingers on the side of her teacup as she thought. "I don't remember her mentioning anyone. You could always start calling the contacts on her cell phone."

"She didn't have a cell phone," said Mel.

"How do you know that?" Dan asked.

"She told me she hated cell phones and wished people would spend more time talking to the people who are right in front of them. It amazed her when cruisers would come in and everybody at the table would be buried in their phone. She used to borrow our phone whenever she needed to make a call."

"Was that often?"

"No, not really. Maybe a little more so this year than in the past, but don't quote me on that. We get so busy, I can't be trusted to remember."

"Did she make any interesting calls?"

"You mean like, *Help, someone's trying to kill me?*" Mel giggled, then stopped. "I'm sorry. That isn't funny. I heard her say she was looking forward to seeing the person she was talking to. I never heard her mention having kids though."

"I don't understand," I said. "She was three weeks late coming home and nobody called to see if she was all right. That's crazy. Someone back home must be missing her."

"Maybe they left a message at the gallery," suggested Mom. "That's the number on the rental agreement, though I assume if they left a message and no one called them back, they'd think to call someone else."

"I have an off-season message asking people to call my cell." I dug my phone out and checked the missed calls. "Artists, mostly. A couple of long-time renters. No numbers I don't recognize, but I'll listen to the voice mails and let you know, Dan."

"Do you have an emergency contact number for her?"

"I might. I ask for one, but her rental application would have been filled out years ago, if Dad even asked her to do one. He'd known her for a long time by then. I don't remember ever asking her to update it."

"You up to taking a look?"

"I could go," Mom offered, starting to get up.

"No, it's okay. I want to go home and take a nap anyway. You and Dad could figure out how I'm going to break all this to the Tilamus. Oh, what about the water, Dan? I can't believe I forgot to ask."

"Still flowing. I turned it off and drained the system before I left."

I put my hand on my chest. "Thank goodness. They're gonna flip out as it is."

"Why? They didn't know her, did they?"

"The Tilamus are never happy to hear bad news," said Mom. "Maybe this will convince them to sell. I'd like to see someone begin to care about that property again. It was a house full of love once."

"Mother, that's so romantic," said Mel with a sigh.

Mom looked embarrassed. "It's simply the truth, Melody."

"You know, on my way over there, I was thinking at this point, there's so much wrong with that house, you'd be better off to tear it down and start over."

"Nonsense, dear. All it would take is for someone to fall in love with it."

"Well, that someone had better have a bucket load of money, Mom." I pushed myself out of my chair and gave her a kiss on the cheek. "Don't worry if I sleep through dinner."

Dan helped me into my coat. I was relieved to see the wind had died down and in spite of the snow on the ground, it felt almost warm. Dan's mind was still on the deplorable condition of the Tilamu house. "Why don't the kids put any money into the house?"

"They're hardly kids, Dan. They're all in their fifties. Aggie might even be sixty by now. You'd have to ask Mom. They were all gone by the time I was born."

"Kids or not, I don't get it. That house is twice as bad inside than out. I was shocked anybody was living there."

"I know, but Mrs. Nash always insisted. It'd break Doc's heart to see the house now, that's for sure."

"Are they just too greedy to spend the money? You'd think they'd want to protect their investment."

"When you split the rent three ways there's not enough money to be greedy about. Truthfully, Dan, I get the impression they don't even like that house."

"Why don't they sell it then? I suppose they wouldn't get much for it."

"Not for the house, but the land is valuable. It's a beautiful location and Doc owned two lots next to the house that he left undeveloped. You could build a great big house that took advantage of the view and it would be worth way more than it is now."

"Why don't you do it? You can't live over your gallery for the rest of your life."

"I like my apartment." I unlocked the door and led Dan inside. "You could buy it and move out of that dump you're living in."

"That dump has been in my family for generations."

"Yes, and you're a fine one to criticize the Tilamus for not putting money into their house. When was the last time you did any improvements to yours?"

"It always looks sad in here off season," said Dan, changing the subject. He looked around the empty exhibit room. Only two paintings remained, huge landscapes by Jack's son, Jonathan Snow, who'd been making a name for himself when he died. I'd shipped everything else back to the artists before I'd been too sick to function.

"It'll fill up again next spring."

"Gallery doing well?"

"We did gangbuster business this year. Johnny's death drove up the value of his paintings and all the extra traffic drove sales of other artists." I felt tears sting my eyes. I'd have given up every dime of profit if it would have brought him back. I shook off the grief and walked briskly toward the office. "I can't imagine next year will be anywhere near as big, but that's all right. I make a decent living and so do the artists I work with. That's saying something."

"What about these?" Dan hadn't moved. He nodded toward the landscapes.

"The one on the left is going on loan to the Alaska State Museums. I'll need to negotiate terms now that I'm feeling better. They'll send a transport company to pick it up."

"Too valuable to ship with Kenny?"

"And way too big. The other will be on permanent display here in the gallery." My voice caught. "Jack didn't want people to forget what a great artist Johnny was."

Dan looked at me, his eyes gently probing. "You miss him."

I spun on my heels, pushing away the pain that made it hard to breathe, and went into my office. Digging through my files steadied me, pulling me back to the safety of my everyday routine. I gave myself more time than I really needed to find the file. But my eyes were clear again when I pulled out a folder and handed it to him.

"Not much here for someone who's been renting from you for so long," Dan observed.

"You know Dad. Working for the state where everything's in triplicate—if it isn't documented, it didn't happen—turned him into a minimalist long before everybody else started worrying about all the trees we were killing in the name of paperwork."

"What made you think she had a thing for Doc?"

I leaned against my desk. "I don't know. Maybe just because they were both alone."

"Couple of old folks in love?" There was a hint of a smile in the corner of his mouth.

"I was a kid, Dan. I was much more interested in my love life than theirs." I stared down at the floor, trying to remember the two of them together. "You'd always see them sitting on one of the benches looking out at the bay. This was way before the cruise ships came, you know. They'd sit out there and watch the fishing boats."

Dan sat down on the couch I keep in the office. "I only knew Mrs. Nash to say hello. Tip of the hat. That sort of thing."

"You really should work on your social skills."

"Very funny. Your family seems pretty convinced she didn't kill herself."

"We've known her forever, that's all. I'm not sure anyone ever thinks someone they know would kill themselves."

"You have a point there. I've been called out to a fair number of suicides and people will tell you how depressed the person was, but they never thought they'd go that far."

"Or they'd been depressed before, but for the last few days of their lives, they seemed happy again." I shivered. "Like they'd made up their mind to go and they were saying goodbye."

"Leaving people with good memories."

"Maybe. I guess we'll never really know. Certainly isn't ever going to be a reason that satisfies the people they leave behind."

We sat there in silence, both lost in our thoughts until I lost track of time. "Help me to know her, Cara. What kind of person was she?"

I pushed away from the desk and started to pace. "I told you before. She was sweet. She'd come by the gallery to pay her rent and see the new paintings I'd put out since the last time. We'd chat, sometimes. If the gallery wasn't too busy. She never imposed if I had customers. She liked watercolors."

"Did she ever buy anything?"

I shook my head. "She was almost apologetic about it, but she told me she had a house full of pretty things back home." I perched on the arm of the couch. "I've been trying to think of things that would help you, to call up memories of things she's said to me and there's so much less there than I thought there would be. I feel like someone important to me is gone and it hurts my heart to think of her, but when I reach out to touch her," I stretched out my hand as if I were grabbing something in the air, "she fades away like a mirage."

"Do I have an emergency contact in there?"

Dan stared at the paper in front of him, then held it up to me. "It's in code."

I sat down next to him and took the folder. "Sorry. I'm the only one who ever looks at these and I'm always in a hurry. This page shows her rent payments. See, I've noted when she came, when she left and when she'd told me she'd be back the next year."

"Is that what those scribbles mean?"

I ignored him, leaning back on the couch. "She had been coming only for the summer but when the cruise ships started, she extended her stay for the entire season. She liked to people watch."

Dan sat back on the couch and I was uncomfortably aware of the heat from his arm pressed against mine. I was debating whether I could move over without him noticing so I almost missed what he said next. "I'm surprised you still have time to manage property."

I got up to put the folder back in the file cabinet. "I don't, but I can't find anyone crazy enough to take over the business."

"What about your dad? Didn't he start the business?"

"Yes, but when I got my real estate license, he handed it over to me. I asked him last year if he'd take it back, but he said he's too old to study for the test to renew his."

Dan laughed, "Bob King is one of those people who'll never be old. He's too smart to take it back. How are you going to make time for your artist in residency project?"

"Who told you about that?" I leaned on my desk, happy to have a little distance between us.

"Jack. He's thrilled that you're turning Johnny's island into a retreat."

I sighed. "Mrs. Nash gave me the idea. She came into the gallery, a couple of weeks before the season ended and we got to talking about a program down in Flagstaff. Of course, it was only a pipe dream then. I didn't think I'd ever have enough money to make it happen."

"Was that the last time you saw her?"

"I've been trying to remember. I think it may have been."

"How did she seem?"

"Not like someone who was planning to kill herself, if that's what you mean. Or someone afraid for her life, for that matter. She was normal, like she always was. We talked about how hard it is to make a living as an artist and she mentioned a program in Arizona that subsidizes artists to spend three months at a retreat doing nothing but making art—painting, sculpture, weaving—whatever medium they work in."

"The way he talks, I thought the whole thing was Jack's idea."

I smiled. "Johnny and I used to talk about how hard it is to paint when you've got to have a day job. He travelled all over the state looking for inspiration. Whenever he stumbled across an artist he thought had promise, he'd refer them to me. When I was first starting out, it was hard to get established artists to exhibit with me so these newbies were my bread and butter. I pretty much have my pick now, but I set aside space every year for emerging artists."

"Were these artists he sent you any good?"

"Johnny had a great eye for talent. When Jack offered me the island, I told him it would make a perfect artist's retreat." I snapped my fingers. "Just like that, he set up a fund to support it and named me the administrator."

"Property manager, business owner and now patron of the arts. You're a regular little tycoon."

"I'm crazy, that's what I am. I don't know how I'm going to get everything done. Cloning. That's what I need. I can go through my emails and see if she mentioned having children."

"Don't bother. I'll contact the police down there. They'll track down her next of kin and let me know where to ship the body."

"I hate referring to Mrs. Nash as 'the body'." I wrapped my arms around myself. "Have you investigated a lot of murders?"

"Much more likely to be a suicide."

"Fine, have you investigated a lot of suicides?"

"Is this a job interview?"

"It's a conversation. Social skills, Dan." I moved toward the door, suddenly embarrassed.

He caught my hand. "I'm sorry. I'm not much good at conversations." He pulled me down beside him on the couch. "To tell you the truth, I haven't investigated much of anything. I was a beat cop, not a detective. I got called out to a few murders and way too many suicides, but I was strictly a grunt, never the man in charge."

"Is that why you insisted on calling the state even though you think she killed herself?"

"A man doesn't want to make a mistake with something like that."

"Do you miss Fairbanks? Coho Bay must seem awfully slow to you."

"I miss the people I worked with, but I don't miss the cold or the darkness. Climate here is way better than Fairbanks too."

"I know what you mean. I was surprised how much colder it got in Anchorage when I lived there."

"Lot more drugs too." His phone beeped and he glanced at the screen. "State's here."

I walked with him to the marina, watching the police boat cutting toward us over the choppy water. "The whole town will be at Mel's dishing dirt. I'll ask around. See if I can find out anything about Mrs. Nash that could help you."

"Don't." He spit out the word, then ran his finger along my cheek to soften his tone. "Don't go asking questions. If it's suicide, whatever you find out won't matter. If it's murder, I don't want you putting yourself in danger."

"Dan, it's been weeks since she died. If it was murder, the killer's long gone."

"I'm not taking any chances." He cupped my face in his hands and kissed me. Light and soft, surprisingly appealing and over way too soon. He pulled away and before I could take another breath, was down the steps and heading for where the police boat was pulling up to the dock. I wondered if my face looked as stunned as I felt.

"I guess you're okay then."

I spun around to see Frank Baker leaning on a lamppost, poorly veiled hostility in his eyes as he watched Dan. Tall and lean, he had what I'd told my sister were romance-novel good looks. In spite of Mom's assumptions, he never seemed to do much more than flirt with me. "What are you doing here? I thought you'd be working on my dad's lumber order."

"I brought him what we had on hand so he and Bent can get started. Walk you home?"

"Yes, thanks. I'm headed back to my place to take a nap. Mom told me she promised you my apartment this winter."

"If it's okay with you. I told her I could stay with Jack."

"She says he's drinking again."

"Jack's always drinking." We crossed the empty street back to the gallery and went around the building.

"Since I'm never going to convince Mom we don't all need to live together this winter, you may as well take the place. It'll be another month though before I can move out."

He took my hand. His was warm but rough from working at the mill. "There's room for two."

"That's not gonna happen."

A lopsided grin spread across his face. "I could sleep on the couch."

An image of Frank, shirtless and clothed only in flannel pajama bottoms, standing at my kitchen counter pouring coffee on a cold winter morning flashed into my head. Despite the cold, it was suddenly uncomfortably warm. I picked up speed, reaching the door to the apartment in record time. "Did you know Mrs. Nash?"

Frank easily kept pace with me. "I heard about you finding her." He caught my hand again and pulled me to a stop. "I'm sorry you had to see a thing like that, Cara."

I looked up at him. His eyes were the color of the bay when it glistens in the summer sunshine. There was worry in the rugged lines of his face. He tugged me closer and I moved into his arms. Somewhere in my brain, alarm bells clanged as I sensed a kiss wasn't all he was looking for. I pulled away and slipped into my apartment, shutting the door and leaning against it, willing my pulse to return to normal. This business of having two men interested in me was tougher than it looked.

Chapter 2

As I'd predicted, the next few days brought locals streaming into Mel's, desperate for a hot meal with a side of gossip. It was a boon for her and Bent, who normally didn't open during the winter except for Sundays after church. I listened intently as I circulated among the tables, refilling cups, taking orders and delivering plates of food, but none of the gossip was worth passing onto Dan. In fact, it seemed our family knew more about Mrs. Nash than anybody in town. Not surprising, but it was disappointing.

It disturbed me to think anyone sitting at Mel's tables could be the cold-blooded killer, so I told myself it was a good thing I had nothing to report when Dan took his usual seat by the window. "You look tired," I said, putting a red and white mug stamped *Coho Bay: a little bit north of normal* on the table.

"Keep me company," he said, casting a glance around the dining room. It was late in the day so there were only a few tables taken.

"Let me put your order in and I'll have lunch with you." I went through the swinging doors into the kitchen where my brother-in-law was scraping the grill. "Dan's here. I need two burgers."

"He must be hungry."

"Very funny. Chips too, if you have any left."

"I could be persuaded to make a fresh batch. I assume you want turkey on yours."

I kissed his cheek. "Much obliged. Where's Mel?"

"Upstairs."

The word was ordinary, but there was worry in his voice. I ran up the steps and pulled up short at the door to Mel's bedroom. It was open and Mom was sitting on the bed, looking as worried as Bent had sounded.

"She's still throwing up?" I asked and Mom made a face. "Holy cow. I am never having a baby."

"You forget all of this when they lay your child in your arms."

"How can anybody forget that?"

"Forget what?" Mel's voice was shaky and her face pale. She stood in the doorway in her pajamas, swaying a bit.

I put my arm around her and helped her to the bed. "Are you sure you're okay, Melly?" I hadn't called her that since she was eight and I was four.

She waved me away and buried her head in the pillow. "If the world would stop spinning that'd be swell."

"Can't help you there." I directed a panicked look at my mother.

She was stroking Mel's hair. "Shoo, Caribou. I'll let you know if we need anything."

I trooped back down the steps and found Bent staring at me when I hit the kitchen. I put my hands up in defeat. "They both swear she's fine."

"That's what they told me before your mother banished me from my own bedroom." He nodded toward two plates, piled high with home-made chips and moose burgers, fresh from the hunt I'd missed while I was sick. Hunting regulations won't let Bent serve wild game, but I wasn't a paying customer and during the off season, nobody cared. "I called Gabby."

"What'd she say?"

"That some women have a harder time than others but she didn't think it was anything to worry about."

"Seems like false advertising to call it morning sickness if you're gonna be sick all day."

Bent laughed. "Well if you find out who to sue, let me know."

I picked up the plates. "You haven't eaten yet. Come join us."

"Need a chaperone?"

"Of course not. It's just Dan."

"Ouch! Don't let him hear you say that, poor guy."

I could feel my face turning red. I flipped my hair, which since I was wearing it in a ponytail just missed putting my eye out. "We're only friends."

"Uh huh. Flip the sign when you get out there, will ya?"

"Sure thing." I pushed into the dining room and dropped the plates off before scooting to the front door. I locked it and turned the sign to *Closed*.

"Well, well, well," said Dan as I sat across from him. "You could have just said you wanted to be alone with me. You didn't have to close the place down."

"Such a funny guy. What have you learned about Mrs. Nash?"

"What should I have learned?"

"Who killed her, for one."

"It was the butler in the lobby with the revolver," he said, picking up his burger.

"There's no lobby in that game, smarty-pants."

"Are you sure?"

"It's a house, not a hotel. Houses don't have lobbies."

"I don't have the autopsy or the lab report yet. Since it's only a possible suicide, it's on the back burner. Could be weeks before they make a determination."

I frowned. "The lab techs thought it was suicide then?"

"Not necessarily. There were a few things they didn't like about the scene either, but not enough to get worked up about."

"You can't hold off that long to investigate, Dan. The trail's already getting cold."

"You were the one who said if it was murder, the killer was long gone. A few more weeks won't matter."

"Did you find her next of kin?"

"Local police are tracking down the family. They didn't find anything in her house so they're putting a notice in the paper."

"That's so sad. What must it be like to be alone in the world? Nobody to love you or miss you when you've gone?"

"I'll let you know."

"You're not alone, Dan. You have family."

"My parents are gone. I have no brothers or sisters. My uncle was the only family I had."

I put my burger down and stared at him. "Crazy ex-wife? Murderous second cousin?"

Dan coughed, half choking. "What makes you say that?"

"If you really would like to go out with me, I'd like to know what I'm getting myself into." I could not believe I said that.

"You must have had some interesting relationships."

I hadn't had much of anything in the way of relationships, but I wasn't admitting it. "You didn't answer."

"What?"

"Ex-wives?"

"I have one. She's not crazy, but not somebody I'd want to invite to a picnic."

"I didn't know you'd been married before."

"Hard to have an ex-wife any other way."

"Such a comedian. How long?"

"Eight years."

"You were married for eight years before you moved here? How old are you, anyway?"

"Why do I not like the sound of that?"

I popped a chip into my mouth before answering. "Sorry. That did sound bad. I mean, I'm not saying you're *old* or anything."

"Yeah, that's much better."

I started to giggle. "I'm sorry. I'm twenty-six, if you want to know."

"I'm thirty-nine."

I couldn't giggle about that. Thirteen years. When I was born, Dan was a teenager. There was almost a whole generation between us. What would we have in common? Did we listen to the same music? Had we read the same books? My parents were always talking about watching Neil Armstrong walk on the moon when they were kids. Could Dan trade stories with them about it? No, wait. Calm down. Dan was old, but he wasn't *that* old.

I looked up to find him watching me and I wondered if he could read my thoughts on my face. Time to change the subject. "I have no idea how to choose the artists for my residency program. I was thinking about going to Anchorage or Juneau and talking with art instructors at the university."

"What's a professor gonna tell you that you don't already know? You sell art every day."

"I know what sells. That doesn't mean I know great art from a hole in the ground."

"Who says? I've seen what museums call art. If I'd found painting like that on the side of a building, I'd be busting somebody for vandalism."

I couldn't help but laugh. "I'm not a fan of modern art either. I like landscapes and wildlife studies and fortunately for me, that's what tourists want to buy."

"So it's not art because it's commercially viable?"

"That's not what I'm saying. The goal of this program is to help artists generate enough work so they will be able to make a living with their art. Commercial viability will be one consideration, but I need to be taken seriously for Johnny's sake. That means I have to attract serious talent and I'm not sure I'm the best judge."

"I thought the point was for them to be able to make a living as an artist. Maybe knowing what sells does make you the best judge."

"I hadn't thought of that."

I ate my chips in silence, not tasting them, which was a disservice to Bent because they were usually really good. Today, they were bland and I had to wash them down with pop. "Maybe that's self-serving. Will people think I'm trying to profit off the residency if I feature these artists in the gallery?"

"I don't think you should care so much what other people think. Trust your own judgment."

I pushed back my chair and gathered the dishes. "I'd better let you get back to work. I'm going to help Dad and Bent upstairs."

"I can help." Dan got up but I waved him off.

"We've got it covered."

Dan opened his mouth to say something, then turned away. "I'll let you know if I hear anything."

I took the dishes into the kitchen and tucked them into the industrial dishwasher. I turned it on, shut off the lights and followed the sound of hammers and saws. Dad and Bent were hard at work framing up the new space. "It's beginning to look like a bedroom."

"That's not good since it's the bathroom we're framing," Dad said, shaking his hammer at me.

"What'd Dan have to say?" asked Bent, looking up from the board he was cutting.

"Not much."

"Why is your face so red?"

"What are you, twelve?" I grabbed a hammer. "What can I help you with, Dad?"

"You could call Frank and see if he's got the next load ready." He gestured toward a depleted pile of lumber.

I pulled out my cell and walked over to the window, where the signal would be stronger. "Dad asked me to check on your ETA."

Frank swore under his breath. "I can bring him a truckload today to tide him over if he's out already."

"He will be by the time you get here. What's wrong?"

There was a long silence. "Let me get the truck loaded. I'll be there as soon as I can."

I relayed the message to Dad and Bent, who looked at each other for a long moment before resuming work. "What am I missing?"

"Jack."

"Gotta be," agreed Bent.

"You mean he's drinking again? That's what Mom told me." I picked up my hammer and went to help Dad with the wall he was working on.

"Terrible thing, seeing a man throw his life away."

"I thought it would help, me starting the residency to honor Johnny."

"Takes something out of a man to bury his son."

"Jack was a drinker long before Johnny died," said Bent.

We worked without further discussion until we ran out of wood. When we hung up our hammers, Dad and I trooped downstairs to wait for Frank, and Bent went to check on Mel. Mom joined us in the dining kitchen, where Dad and I were digging into leftover apple pie.

"Last pie of the season, Marcie. Pull up a chair and I'll cut you a piece."

"How's Mel?" I asked as Mom sat down. Her face was grim.

"Still throwing up. Thank you, Robert. I have a call into rural health. Gabby thinks she may need to go to Juneau."

I dropped my fork. Little fingers of fear crept into me. Having a baby was supposed to be the most natural thing a woman could do. "Bent said Gabby told him she was fine."

"She didn't want to worry him. We've been hoping it would pass."

"She's going to be all right, though?"

Mom's voice was reassuring. "Of course. She just needs to get the nausea under control and I'm concerned about her becoming dehydrated. If we had a doctor here, it would be different."

"Clem's trying, Marcie."

"He's not trying hard enough. Cara could have died from pneumonia and Melody should be able to go three blocks to the clinic and get whatever she needs, not risk her life going all the way to Juneau."

"You're being a bit dramatic, don't you think Marcie?"

Mom got up and started pacing, her anxiety making me more nervous by the minute. "What if she has to stay in Juneau until the baby comes? Away from her everyone she loves. Robert, it's just not right."

"I thought the new building was supposed to finally land us a doctor." There had been no doctor in Coho Bay since Doc died, despite my mother's constant nagging. Once the cruise ship money started flowing, she had persuaded them to build a clinic but they'd drawn the line at offering financial incentives. Now we have a lovely, but empty, clinic but the battle to build it had been so heated, nobody wanted to revisit incentivizing a doctor.

Mom spun around and her words came out in rapid fire. "They expect someone to come all the way out here for nothing more than tuition forgiveness from the state. I keep telling Solokov, he has to sweeten the pot. We're competing against every other rural community in Alaska."

My father had heard her arguments many times. "If they found someone who was interested, I'm sure Clem would negotiate."

"How can you negotiate when nobody will even look twice? I've got a good mind to run against that idiot when he comes up for re-election."

I put down the fork I'd just picked up. "Nobody's ever run against Mayor Solokov."

"Then it's high time somebody did."

"But he's been mayor as long as I can remember."

"Longer than we've lived here," supplied my father.

"Yes, and his father was mayor before him, but this is a democracy not a fiefdom. I say, break the back of the good old boy network if it's not going to put the needs of the citizens first!"

My father and I sat staring at each other in stunned silence. When she put her mind to something, my mother was an irresistible force and I wouldn't want to be an immovable object in her path. I wasn't sure she would actually run against Solokov, and if she did, I had no idea whether anyone would break tradition and vote for her, but by the fire in her eyes, I wouldn't bet against her.

***

Mom had gone back upstairs to sit with Mel by the time Frank arrived. I put on my coat and went out to help him haul it in while Dad went upstairs to decide where to put the boards since we needed to frame out the area where they'd piled the first load. Frank was loosening the straps that bound the wood to the trailer when I made it outside. What was it about him that made my blood pressure soar every time I saw him? His good looks were hidden under a layer of sawdust and sweat which coated his hair, face, coat and jeans but he still had the same effect on me.

I took a deep breath to settle myself. "What happened to you?"

"What do you mean?"

"You look like you took a sawdust bath." I grabbed the latch on one of the straps and started working it free.

Frank looked down at his soiled clothes and brushed at his coat. Since his gloves were wet from the snow on the tarp that covered the wood, the result was more comedic than clean. "You try cutting a tree into board feet and see how you look."

He reached for my hand but I pulled away. My mind didn't want to be covered in sawdust but my rebellious body didn't care. "We have to get this wood inside before it gets soaked."

"It'll dry." Like the romance novel hero I'd always pictured him, Frank had a huskiness in his voice that sent the world into slow motion. He bent to kiss me and the scent of rugged lumberman filled my senses. Lumber. Sawdust. I jerked away from him and sneezed. And sneezed and sneezed!

The romantic mood was shattered, but I wasn't the one laughing. Bent's booming laughter and raucous applause brought me resoundingly back down to earth. Frank stood beside the trailer, no longer looking like a romantic hero, and not only was he not laughing, he looked annoyed. Maybe it was Bent who exasperated him and not my reaction to his kiss.

"You two want to be alone?" Bent asked as soon as he could talk.

I resumed my fight with the strap. "I won't remind you how sappy you and Mel can be."

Bent pulled off my hat and ruffled my hair. "Love is a many splendored thing, little sister."

I couldn't correct Bent without hurting Frank so I said nothing. I kept my eyes on the strap and my thoughts on the job at hand. My pulse was still racing but I was able to blame it on climbing a steep flight of stairs carrying a stack of ten foot two-by-fours. Bent and Frank maneuvered their loads single-handedly but mine bounced on the hand rail, bringing my dad down to take one end and help me wrestle it the rest of the way up the stairs.

Mel was sitting by the window on the far side of the unfinished space, looking a little livelier. By the time we finished, the four of us collapsed in a heap at her feet. Bent leaned back against her legs while Dad and I propped each other up and Frank slouched against the cold outer wall. Mom had gone down to "rustle up a little something" which I hoped meant raiding leftovers and not trying to cook. My mother was a biologist with a brilliant scientific mind but it didn't translate well to the kitchen.

"It's going to be beautiful, Dad," said Mel. "Have you got enough lumber now?"

"One way to know for sure, eh Bent?" He pushed himself onto his feet and ambled over to what would be my bedroom first, but would eventually become the baby's room. Bent followed, dropping a kiss on Mel's face and patting the top of my head. Frank gave me a long look, then joined Dad and Bent.

"Looks like somebody's been getting a little action." Mel kept her voice low so the men wouldn't hear.

My cheeks burned. Someday, I needed to learn how to control that reaction. It was bad enough having beet red hair without my face burning too. "I'm sorry you've been so sick."

"Mother's getting worried but Gabby's telling me it's nothing serious. I swear, I thought they were going to punch each other out over it."

"Must be hard on Gabby being the only person in town with any medical training."

"Don't you start. Mother's bad enough. It hurts Gabby's feelings."

"It shouldn't. We do need a doctor and not because Gabby isn't good at what she does. She brought me into the world, after all. Doc always said she was better at babies than he'd ever be."

"You're changing the subject."

"No I wasn't. I was talking about morning sickness."

"I was talking about Frank. And Dan. Cara, you can't keep playing them against each other. It isn't fair."

"What do you mean? I'm not officially dating either of them. Frank's been working and Dan…"

"Dan's been eating every meal here."

"You can't pin that on me. Dan's been eating every meal here since you opened. I don't think he can cook."

Mel huffed and stared out the window. "The way Mother makes it sound—"

"You've been talking about me with Mom?" I interrupted her.

"She's been doing most of the talking. I've been puking my guts out. I should warn you, she's rooting for Frank."

"Why Frank?"

"She thinks Dan's too old for you. She has a point, Cara. Thirteen years is a long time."

"How did you know Dan's age but I didn't? How old is Frank?"

"I'm not sure, but younger than Dan."

"He's an outsider."

"I know. You'd think that would be a strike against him but she thinks there's something shady about Dan."

I laughed, drawing the attention of the men on the other side of the room. I waved and they went back to work. "Dan's a cop. He's been a cop all his life. It's all he's ever wanted to do, just like his uncle. There's nothing shady about Dan."

Mel looked sharply at me. "If you like Dan so much, why are you stringing Frank along?"

I drew my legs up and wrapped my arms around them, resting my chin on my knees. "I'm not stringing anybody along. I like Frank too."

"You can't have both of them."

"Mel, I don't have either of them yet. They both seem interested, but nobody's come out and said anything. Besides, why do I have to choose right now? I've gone my whole life with guys not giving me a second look and now that I've suddenly got two eligible, decent-looking, employed men showing an interest in me, why do I have to choose?"

Mel nudged me to turn my back to her and began to braid my hair. I watched the men working, warm enough now that they'd shed their coats. Bent was all muscle in a compact package and I wondered, not for the first time, what he'd done in the Navy besides cook. Frank was tall and lean with fluid movements that almost made up for his obvious lack of building knowledge. My father was taller than both of them. I'd gotten my height from him, while Mel had inherited our mother's beauty. I squinted, trying to replace Frank with Dan in my mind and wondering which man would declare himself first. Or would I manage to scare both of them away, as I had the few other man I'd dated.

Thinking about Dan brought the thought of Mrs. Nash's lifeless body sweeping over me in a cold wave. I screwed my eyes shut and shook my head, trying to clear that image from my mind. "What's wrong, Cara?" Mel asked as she struggled to recapture my hair.

"I can't stop seeing her." I buried my head against my knees again but she was still there, faceless, frozen, frightening.

Mel put her head against mine. Her hands were gentle on my shoulders, radiating compassion. "I'm sorry, Cara," she whispered.

I sniffed, fighting the urge to cry. "It makes me sad to think how little I really knew about her. What was she like when she wasn't in Coho Bay? Dan says the Flagstaff police haven't found any family yet. They have to put an ad in the paper, like she was a lost dog or something."

"If she had any children, I never heard her talk about them. My baby isn't even born yet, and you can't get me to shut up about her."

"Her? How do you know it's a girl?"

"I don't. Bent and I have a bet. If it's a boy, he gets to pick the name but I get to name a girl."

"What if he picks a terrible name?"

"Like what?"

"Bentley Junior."

Mel laughed. "Bent's already a junior. Our baby would be the third."

"B-three? Yeah, you'd better hope it's a girl."

"I only care that the baby is healthy." She patted her belly. "Nothing else matters."

"What name did you pick out?"

"You'll find out as soon as we have a girl."

"How many kids do you want to have?"

Mel didn't answer. "Does Dan have any idea who killed her?"

"He thinks it's probably suicide."

"But he called in the state. He must think there's something fishy about it."

"He hasn't got a lot of experience investigating suspicious deaths and wanted a second opinion. I guess he didn't think that would be a good enough reason get the mayor to spend the money."

"You'd think it was Clem's money, the way he holds onto it. Why would Mrs. Nash kill herself?"

I had no chance to answer. Dad put down his hammer and called over to us. "I hear Marcie ringing the dinner bell. Let's go see what she found."

He headed toward the steps. Bent put his arm around Mel, who'd risen from her chair and Frank put out a hand to me. He pulled me to my feet, bringing my face uncomfortably close to his. My nose started to tickle again from the sawdust and I pulled away. "I'm starved," I mumbled and ducked around Mel and Bent, who were moving more slowly. I was rarely hungry enough to eat my mother's cooking, but right now it seemed the lesser of two evils.

Chapter 3

"You're not gonna believe it."

I looked up from the book I was reading as Dan slid onto a chair across the table from me. I was taking a break from the construction and since Mel's was closed, I had my feet up on the chair beside me and was hip-deep in one of my favorite Agatha Christie novels. "I'm sorry," I said, forcibly pulling myself out of St. Mary Mead and staring at him blackly. "What won't I believe?"

"Got any more of those?" He gestured at the cinnamon roll, half-eaten on my plate.

I slipped in a bookmark. "It's a couple of days old. Mel doesn't bake much in the off season."

He was looking at the book when I put the plate down. "You didn't like the ones I sent over while you were sick?"

"I finished them."

"All of them? There must have been fifteen books."

"Your point being? What won't I believe?"

He shook his head and picked up a fork. "I'm not taking Mrs. Nash's body home to Arizona."

"You were going to take her home personally? Did the mayor know about this?"

"Clem's not a bad guy. I just didn't like the idea of her going back in a cargo hold like somebody's lost luggage."

"That's sweet. What made you change your mind?"

"She didn't want to go."

"She told you that? You're speaking to the dead now?"

He smiled, enjoying himself. "Only the near dead. I had a call from her lawyer this morning."

"She had a lawyer?"

"Who had a lawyer? Hello, Daniel. You two won't mind if I join you."

I put my hand on my heart. "Sheesh, Mom, make some noise when you sneak up on people. I coulda had a heart attack."

"You're far too young for that, Caribou." She pushed my feet off the chair and sat down next to me, putting her tea cup on the table in front of her. "Go on. Who had a lawyer?"

"Mrs. Nash. Dan said she doesn't want to go back to Arizona."

My mother raised an eyebrow at him. "Is that so?"

"Yes, ma'am. Seems she wanted to be buried right here in Coho Bay."

"Then it had to be suicide, if she left instructions like that for her attorney." I pushed my half-eaten cinnamon roll away. I didn't like thinking that someone I'd liked had chosen to die.

My mother pulled over my plate and grabbed a fork from an adjoining table. "I would think she left burial instructions in her will."

"Two points for the lady," said Dan. "The lawyer called the local P.D. and they told him to call me."

"We'll have a nice funeral for Mrs. Nash. When will they release her body, Daniel?"

"She's ready now. I just have to pick her up." He looked at me. "Want to run me up to Juneau?"

I made a face. "That won't be a fun trip." At his look of disappointment, I added, "but I could go, if you think Dad and Bent can spare me, Mom."

She gave me a long look. "You'd be better off riding with Kenny. He has a bigger boat than we do and he'll be making a mail run tomorrow."

"Good idea, Marcie. Kenny's set up to haul freight."

"I don't want to think of Mrs. Nash as freight," I said.

"Well, you certainly wouldn't want to have the coffin in the cabin with you." I looked sharply at her. I thought I detected a slight hint of a smile, but I wasn't sure enough to call her on it.

"I guess you're off the hook, Cara. I'll head out tomorrow with Kenny." Dan pushed away his empty plate and took a drink of his coffee. "The attorney wants you to call him."

"Me? Why?"

Dan pushed a scrap of paper over to me with the name Thomas Clarke and a phone number written on it. "No idea, but if you feel like calling him now, I'm curious."

"Me too," said my mother, getting up to refill our coffee and fetch more hot water for her tea.

"That makes three of us." I pulled out my cell phone and dialed the number. After telling a polite woman who answered who I was and why I was calling, she put me through to Mr. Clarke.

"Ms. King, thank you for calling."

"Dan tells me Mrs. Nash wanted to be buried here."

"Yes, she left specific instructions to that effect. Mr. Simmons thought your family might be willing to spearhead the arrangements."

"Of course, we'd be happy to do that. Was that what you needed to speak with me about?"

"In part. If you would arrange for her transportation and burial and have the bills sent to my office, I'll make sure they are paid out of the proceeds from her estate."

"Forgive me, but I didn't even know she had an estate."

"Technically, everyone has an estate, Ms. King. Mrs. Nash was not a wealthy woman, but she did have property here and in Coho Bay that will pass to her heirs."

"She has family then? We weren't sure."

"She has a granddaughter."

"I wonder if she'll want to come to the funeral. I know it's a long way, but I should invite her, just the same."

"I'll check with her and let you know."

"Wait, did you say Mrs. Nash had property in Coho Bay?" Mom and Dan exchanged surprised looks.

"Yes. That's the other thing I wanted to speak with you about. Mr. Simmons tells me you are the only licensed real estate agent in the area?"

"As far as I know. We don't have many sales around here."

"I suspect Mrs. Nash's granddaughter will want to liquidate her property in Alaska. I haven't spoken with her yet, but regardless, I will need a current assessment of the property's value for probate."

"I'd be happy to do that for you. Could you tell me where the property is? I wasn't aware she owned anything here."

"She referred to it in her will as *The Tilamu House*. When I asked for an address, she told me that was as much address as anyone in Coho Bay ever needed. Ms. King? Are you still there?"

I'd dropped the phone so I picked it up. "Yes. Yes, I'm sorry."

"Does that address make sense to you?"

"Yes it does. I know exactly where the property is."

"Wonderful. I left my contact information with Mr. Simmons. Let me know when you have the assessment and I'll be in touch about the granddaughter's wishes regarding the funeral." He gave me the granddaughter's name and wished me a good day.

I hope I remembered to thank him before the phone disconnected. I wasn't quite sure. I was so stunned at the thought of Mrs. Nash actually owning the Tilamu house that I wasn't sure of anything until my mother shook me to get my attention.

"Caribou, what on earth? What did he say?"

"Mrs. Nash owned property in Coho Bay?" asked Dan.

"He said she owned the Tilamu house."

"What?" Dan's voice was loud and it echoed in the empty dining room.

"That's impossible," said my mother. "I thought you talked to Alex yesterday."

"I did."

"Alex?" asked Dan.

"Alex Tilamu. I had to do something about the house. I didn't want to clean it up if he's just going to tear it down and sell the land in the spring."

"But he doesn't own the house after all?"

"This is the first I've heard of it, Daniel. What did Alex have to say?"

"He said he'd talk to his sisters and let me know. There has to be some mistake, Mom. The Tilamus have always owned that property. Mrs. Nash has been paying them rent for six years. Who would do that, then turn around and tell her attorney the house was hers?"

"Caribou, you're going to have to pull the title on that house and send a copy to Mr. Clarke."

"I guess I'll be going to Juneau with you and Kenny after all, Dan."

***

"I miss drywall."

My father laughed as he hammered a nail into his end of the wooden plank we were using as paneling in the family room. We were trying to get as much done as possible today since I would be gone tomorrow. "You hate hanging drywall."

"Not as much as I hate this stuff." I put a couple of nails into my end of the plank and we both took a step toward each other to drive more nails in along the next stud. I put my finger through a gap between planks, created by a missing knothole. "This isn't very private for the bedroom on the other side of this wall."

"We'll drywall the bedroom in the spring. This'll work for now. Besides, I think it looks nicer than drywall. I might do a wall or two of the stuff when we build the new house."

"What new house?"

He looked at me, a bit sheepishly. "Forget I said that."

"Dad, you and Mom aren't seriously considering building next door, are you?" My parents owned the vacant lot behind Mel's place and I'd kidded her that they might build onto the restaurant once they found out she was expecting their first grandchild. I hadn't liked the pallor that had appeared on her face so I hadn't brought it up again.

We finished the plank and he brought another one from the pile and lined it up. He started the first nail before he spoke. "Mel would hate the idea, wouldn't she?"

"She doesn't know yet?"

"We're only in the talking about it stage." He finished his end and waited while I drove in two nails and we took our step toward the middle. "You know how much I love the log house, but your mother..."

"You don't have to explain it to me." We did two more planks as I mulled over an idea. "Why don't you take my apartment? I could live in my cabin." Mel and I both had cabins near my parents' log home. She hadn't lived in hers since she married Bent, but I usually moved out to mine every winter.

"You can't live all the way out there during the season. You'd need a car."

"You don't have a car."

"I don't work in town."

We finished the wall and moved to the next one. "Let's think on it," Dad said as we paneled around the window. "Lots of time between now and spring."

My phone rang and Dad went downstairs to get us something to drink while I answered it. The voice sounded tired and there was the sound of voices in the background. "Yes, this is Caribou King. Who is this?"

"I'm Angela Nash's granddaughter, Olivia Jordan."

"Dr. Jordan, thank you for calling. I wanted to speak with you about the funeral. I hope you know how much we all loved your grandmother."

"I know she loved your family, and she loved Coho Bay. She talked about it so much, I feel as though I've already been there."

"I hope you will be here soon. We need to do the burial before the ground freezes, but the memorial service can be scheduled whenever it's convenient for you."

"You're very kind. I talked to my boss and he's giving me compassionate leave. I can get a flight out tomorrow morning and be in Juneau by the morning after. The airline said that's as close as they can get me. Is there a ferry or something I catch from there?"

"I was planning on going to Juneau tomorrow. I'll talk to Kenny and see if we can delay a day, then you can catch a ride with us."

"That's perfect! Oh, shoot. They're paging me to the ER. I'll call you when I get there." The line went dead and I wondered if I should have told Olivia why I was going to town and what our cargo would be on the trip home. Probably a better conversation to have face to face, I decided. I thumbed through my contacts and called Dan.

"We're gonna have to make our day trip day later," I told him. "That is, if you think it'll be all right with Kenny."

"It's okay by me, but is there a problem?"

"Mrs. Nash's granddaughter is coming for the funeral and will be flying in day after tomorrow. I thought it would be easier to pick her up than to have her wait for the next ferry."

"Why don't you and I take your boat and stay over in Juneau? Kenny can take Mrs. Nash back with him tomorrow. That way you've got time to pull the title and Olivia Jordan doesn't have to spend three hours in a boat with her grandmother's body and a pack of strangers."

"Dan Simmons, you're a good man."

"Don't let it get around."

I laughed and hung up the phone. Hearing footsteps in the hallway, I pushed away from the window and went to tell Dad about the change in plans. The words caught in my throat when I saw Frank following behind him, carrying two glasses of pop. He handed me one and kissed me on the cheek, putting his arm around my waist. I stood awkwardly, feeling my cheeks burning.

"Who was that, honey?" asked Dad, dropping into the chair by the window.

I slipped away from Frank and went to stand beside Dad. Frank's expression was somewhere between puzzled and annoyed. "Olivia Jordan, Mrs. Nash's granddaughter. She's coming for the funeral."

"Really? It's good she could get away on short notice."

"They're giving her a few days off for compassionate leave."

"Don't let your mother find out she's a doctor or she'll figure out a way to get her to stay before she even steps off the boat."

"That's not a bad idea," said Frank, joining us. "We need a doctor."

We stood on either side of my dad and his head went back and forth between us as we talked, as though he were watching a tennis match. "I don't know what kind of doctor Olivia is," I reminded him. "She could be a plastic surgeon for all we know."

Frank rubbed a scar that ran along the line of his chin. "I could use a little work." The corner of his mouth curved up and he winked at me.

"When's she getting here?" asked Dad.

"Day after tomorrow."

"Maybe Kenny can put off your trip for a day so you can pick her up."

"What trip?" asked Frank.

I didn't want to answer so Dad filled him in. "Cara's going to Juneau to pull some title paperwork on a property. Dan's riding up with Kenny to get Mrs. Nash's body. Seems she left instructions she wanted to be buried in Coho Bay."

"You can't get that information online?"

"Not always, especially with older properties and there are some questions about the chain of ownership on this one. I thought it would be a good idea to do a more extensive title search than I can do online and get certified copies of the deed."

"No need for you to ride around with a dead body. The mill's shut down for the winter. I'd be happy to keep you company."

I spared a pleading look at my dad, who misread my signal. "Hey, Cara, that's a good idea. Then Olivia can ride back with you two instead of going with the body. That'd be hard on anyone."

"Actually, Kenny is going to pick up Mrs. Nash tomorrow as planned. I'm going to bring Dr. Jordan home in our boat."

"Who is Dr. Jordan?" asked my mother, interrupting the question Frank had begun to ask. Thank you, God, for your perfect sense of timing.

"Olivia Jordan. She's Mrs. Nash's granddaughter and she's coming here for the funeral. I'm going to pick her up at the airport day after tomorrow."

"Why don't you speak with Kenneth and Daniel about putting the trip off for a day?"

Oh Mom, you were doing so well. "You and I should put our heads together, Mom," I said, locking arms with her and practically dragging her out of the room. "We've got a funeral to plan, double quick. Let's see if Mel wants to help."

I pulled her into the bedroom, where Mel was sitting in a rocking chair by the window, and shut the door. I dropped Mom's arm and dropped onto the bed. A chain of soft yellow yarn was emerging from Mel's knitting needles and running into her lap. "I didn't know you could knit."

Mel's brows were knotted in concentration and she answered without looking up. "Mother's teaching me."

"Mom knits?"

"I do many things, young lady, which you know nothing about. Now, what was the meaning of that charade?"

"What? Oh shoot. I think I dropped a stitch."

"Your sister was having a perfectly ordinary conversation with your father and Franklin but when I came in, she threw herself at me and pulled me in here claiming we had to plan Mrs. Nash's funeral, right now, this instant."

Mel stopped trying to knit and looked up at me. "Why did you do that?"

"It's nothing. Mrs. Nash's granddaughter—"

"The doctor," said Mom.

"She's a doctor?" asked Mel.

"Yes, but I don't know what kind of doctor so don't ask. Anyway, she's coming for the funeral day after tomorrow."

"We're having the funeral day after tomorrow?" asked Mel. "Mom, she's right. We'd better call the ladies at the church and see if we can pull something together."

"I'm picking her up day after tomorrow," I corrected, "though I don't think she has much time off."

"I will take care of the funeral," said Mom. "What I'm more interested in is why you hustled me out of there before I'd hardly set foot in the room."

"Yeah, Cara. What's up with that?"

I put my head on my hands. "Because I didn't want to go into great detail in front of Frank about a trip I'm taking with Dan. Now do you two understand?"

"You'd better call Dan and reschedule since Olivia's not getting in until day after tomorrow," said Mel.

"Is there a broken record in this house? Dan and I will follow Kenny up in our boat tomorrow because Dan has to sign for the body. Kenny will bring Mrs. Nash back tomorrow and Dan and I will stay in Juneau to do the title search on the Tilamu house. We'll bring Olivia back with us so she doesn't have to spend three hours in a boat staring at her grandmother's coffin."

Mel smiled. "I can see why you didn't want to say that in front of Frank."

"Caribou, I think you're making a mistake."

"Mom, it's not what you're thinking. I'm not doing this so I can sleep with Dan."

"That's disappointing, but that's not the mistake to which I was referring."

"What?" Mel and I said in unison.

"What is disappointing or what is the mistake?"

"Both," I said.

"I'm disappointed that you are not more willing to explore your sexuality, Caribou. A woman should not restrict herself until she is ready to commit. While you're young and unencumbered, you should enjoy yourself."

"I'm sorry you asked, Cara." Mel sat back in her rocker, looking a little green and I didn't think it was the morning sickness this time.

"Mom, the last thing I want to talk to you about is my sexual explorations."

"Because there haven't been any," added Mel.

"You're not helping."

"That's my point," said Mom. "You need to spread your wings. With proper protection, of course. I assume you're aware of the options available to you and that you are aware that using oral birth control does not protect you from sexually transmitted disease."

Now I was turning green, but Mel had started to giggle. "If that's the disappointment, what's the mistake?"

"I don't want to know."

"Daniel is not the right man for you, Caribou."

"Let me get this straight. You think I should have sex with him as long as I dump him like a rock afterward. Is that what you're telling me?"

"Laugh all you want, but Franklin is a much better match for you and you risk driving him away by being openly flirtatious with Daniel."

"You want her to sleep with Dan but not flirt with him, Mother?"

"This conversation stops right now. Mom, I appreciate your... openness, but I don't want to play games with either of these guys, so you and Mel need to butt out."

"Hey, don't tar me with the same brush," Mel protested, throwing up her hands. "You're the one who ran in here."

"Fine. Now that we have that settled, let's plan a funeral."

"Consider it done," said Mom. "Let's think about how to persuade Dr. Jordan to move to Coho Bay."

Chapter 4

The wind that had been showering us with snow for weeks stilled sometime during the night and by the time Dan and I cast off the next morning, the waters were calm and the sun promised as warm a trip as we could hope for in late October. Kenny had a bigger, faster boat than my family, so we'd agreed he would set off an hour later, giving Dan and me the bay to ourselves. I chugged along slowly, letting the engine warm up, getting the feel for how it responded. Our family's old boat, held together with duct tape, had finally given up the ghost at the end of the season so when Jack offered me Johnny's boat, I'd jumped at the chance.

Drawing even with the tiny island where Johnny had built the home that would become the artist's retreat, I felt the familiar tug that enveloped me whenever I thought about my childhood friend. We'd grown up together, and I'd always thought there would be more than friendship someday, but he'd married someone else. I'd lost what I'd never really had but that didn't completely dull the pain.

Dan was leaning against the railing, looking out at the bay. The lines etched on his face told a story, if only I could read it. Was it laughter around his eyes and mouth or were they scars from what he'd seen on the job? It had horrified me to find Mrs. Nash's body. What must it have been for Dan to have seen so many? Maybe it was easier if you hadn't known the person but I didn't think I could do a job where standing guard over dead bodies was a regular occurrence.

As if he sensed my eyes on him, he turned, animating the lines with his smile. "Shall we see what this baby can do?"

I grinned back at him and opened the throttle, leaving Johnny's island behind and punching through the mouth of the bay into the waters of the Inside Passage. The pilot station was protected by a three-sided canvas cover, open behind us but sheltered from the worst of the wind and weather. The cover kept out the spray, much appreciated considering the chill in the air, but it did nothing to dampen the roar of the engine as I revved up.

I love driving a boat. Every worry was driven out by the sheer joy of being on open water, harnessing the force of a motor twice as powerful as anything I'd driven before. Movement off our port side caught my eye and I pointed out the pod of dolphins. They were keeping pace easily, leaping in and out of the water, inviting us to play.

The hours passed in a wink and long before I was ready to throttle down, we arrived at the Gastineau Channel that leads to Juneau. "You know," I said as I slowed to the required speed, "if I were going to live anyplace but Coho Bay, I think it would be here."

"Why is that?" Dan was perched on the seat beside me, tipping up his metal travel mug to drain the last of his coffee. We hadn't talked much during the trip since the engine noise made conversation a challenge.

I watched a red tram disappear into the clouds covering Mount Roberts and considered. Juneau is split by the channel, with a bridge between the more commercial mainland and the primarily residential Douglas Island. Cruise ships flock to Juneau all summer, four or more ships a day, disgorging thousands more passengers than Coho Bay would ever see. When Coho Bay won our first cruise ship contract, but before the ships started coming, I worked in a gallery here to learn the trade. It had amazed me that while chaos reigned on Marine Way, two or three blocks away there was peace with nary a tourist in sight. I never understood why, when they had an entire city stretched out before them, most cruisers stuck to a few blocks full of gift shops and galleries.

"I loved Juneau when I lived here," I answered as I steered the boat into the public marina. "The mountains are breathtaking, and the black tulips in the medians are gorgeous. I've been pestering the merchant association to put in a flower garden in that open space beside the clinic. We could have benches and tables where people could eat a picnic lunch. I seem to be the only one who thinks it's a good idea."

"It would call attention to the fact that we have a clinic with no doctor."

"Mom's planning to recruit Dr. Jordan." We pulled up to an empty berth and Dan jumped out to tie up the boat. I shut off the engine and joined him on the dock.

"I wouldn't count your mother out. She usually gets people to do what she wants."

"That is the story of my life, Dan."

***

We took a cab to the morgue and I waited while Dan spoke with the coroner and signed for the body to be released. The coffin, a plain wooden box like something out of an old Western, was loaded into the corner's van and we rode with the technician to the dock where Kenny waited. I looked to see what saying he would have chosen for his ball cap. He had a surprisingly large collection and always seemed to have something appropriate. Today his hat was black with gold letters that said, *Heaven Bound*.

I stood watching the men load the coffin into the hold. Kenny's boat started life as a fishing vessel, which was how he'd originally made his living. Over the years, the fishing boats were forced to go further and further out to sea and one Sunday after church, Kenny had announced he was done. He hung up his nets and never fished commercially again. At least, that was the story my father told. I had often wondered if there weren't more to it.

Whatever his reason, he'd converted the boat to freight and landed contracts with the postal service and various shipping companies to service the people in and around Coho Bay. He made daily trips during the season and usually made it to Juneau once or twice a week off season. I couldn't do business without him, since cruisers preferred to have art shipped to them at home.

Once the sad task was done and Kenny was on his way home, Dan and I caught a ride with the technician as far as the center of town. We walked to our hotel from there and dropped our overnight bags in the rooms Tammy had reserved for us. The little matchmaker had made sure we had adjoining rooms, so I checked to make sure the door between us was locked before rejoining Dan in the hallway.

"Do we have time for lunch?" he asked.

I checked the time on my phone. "Two thirteen, no wonder I'm starving. Where do you want to go?"

"You're the expert. What's good?"

"There's a little hole in the wall down the street from the capital. It has the best crab cakes in the world."

"Don't let Bent hear you say that." He held out his arm for me and we headed into the late afternoon sun, which had burned the clouds off the mountain. Crowds were sparse since the tourist season was over and the legislative session wouldn't begin until January.

BeBe's Crab Shack was just as I remembered it, long and narrow, with room for only one table by the window, which was fortunately empty, though so were most of the tables since we were so far past the lunch rush. A waitress waved at us as we came in so we hung our coats on the backs of our chairs and settled into do a little people-watching. Once we had our coffee cups filled and our orders placed, Dan stretched out his legs and gave me a long look. "What?" I asked, suddenly self-conscious.

"Nothing. It's just... Nah, you'll think I'm nuts."

"I already know that." I teased him. *Definitely laugh lines,* I thought, at least most of them were. There were a few his smile didn't reach, especially around his eyes.

"This just isn't what I'd pictured for our first date."

"This isn't a date."

"You plus me plus food. Sounds like a date."

"If you plus me plus food is all it takes to make a date, we've been dating for years at Mel's." I liked the sound of his laughter.

"That takes the pressure off then. Here, I've been wondering what I could do to impress you."

I crossed my arms on the table. "Do you need to impress me?"

The waitress appeared with two plates heaped with crab cakes and home-cut fries, so Dan waited until she'd gone to answer. "I'm not very good at dating."

"You were married." I inhaled the heavenly aroma of crab and spices, making my head spin and my mouth water.

"Long time ago."

I waited, but he didn't elaborate. "And?"

He picked up his fork. "And it didn't work out."

"You must have been young."

"Right out of high school."

He started eating. Clearly, the past wasn't high on his list of conversation starters. I suppose I couldn't blame him. If I had been married and divorced, even if it was amicable, I wasn't sure I'd want to talk about it on a first date. "So what do you do for fun?"

He set down his fork and looked out at the sidewalk. "Same as anybody, I guess."

"You hunt?"

"I used to. Now I mostly stick to fishing. Don't tell Clem, though. I don't think he'd appreciate me dropping a line while I'm supposed to be on patrol." He winked at me, explaining one of the wrinkles in the corner of his eyes.

"You must like to read. Those books you gave me were dog-eared."

"They were that way when I bought 'em. We can stop at the used bookstore after lunch, if you want."

Reading was probably the only thing I liked better than crab cakes, but it could be an expensive habit. "I'd love to! How'd you know my supply was running low?"

"The way you read? You might want to get yourself a back-up hobby. Pace yourself."

"I have lots of hobbies to keep me busy in the off season."

"Like?"

"Snowmobiling, snow shoeing, hunting. I missed that this year. Fortunately, Bent went out with Dad and filled the freezer."

He finished his crab and sat back in his chair. "Other than your first year of college, have you always lived in Alaska?"

"Born and raised. My folks started out in Anchorage, but they jumped at the chance to move south. I was born in a tent while they were building their log house."

"Good thing you're a June baby."

"I know, huh? I've only heard the stories but Mel remembers life in the tent."

"It would be tough to forget spending an Alaskan winter in a pup tent."

"Oh, come on. It was a wall tent, built to withstand the cold, complete with wood stove. We still use it as a base camp for long hunts."

Dan grinned and I tossed a napkin at him. He checked his watch and reached for his billfold. "We'd better get moving if we're gonna get your title search done before the records office closes."

I followed him out to the sidewalk. "What did the coroner have to say?"

"Gunshot wound from undetermined source."

"I could have told you that. Was it murder or suicide?"

"It means that it could have been either. There was some gunshot residue on her hand. Not as much as you'd expect, though it might have come off in the snow. She was shot at very close range but she didn't hold the gun against her head as most suicides do."

"She might have changed her mind, or started to, maybe the gun had a smoother trigger pull than she expected. I doubt she would have fired it very often before... that day."

"Possibly."

"So what are you going to do now?"

We'd reached the building that housed the state records office. Dan pulled the door open for me. "What do you think?"

"Whatever it is cops do to figure these things out. Investigate."

"I won't get very far with nothing to go on. Don't look at me like that. When the lab boys get me their report, I'll see whether they think anyone else was in the house. Until then, there's not much I can do."

We found the Office of Land Registry and waited for the clerk to finish her phone call. The room smelled like dust with an undertone of tobacco. The source of the latter hung up the phone and sidled over to us. I wondered how many packs she'd gone through at lunch for the scent to make my eyes water three hours later. She ignored me and looked at Dan expectantly, strike two for cigarette lady.

"I'm doing a title search on a property in Coho Bay," I started.

Cigarette lady frowned, lengthening the tendrils of lipstick that were bleeding up her tell-tale smoker's wrinkles, still keeping her eyes on Dan. "Address?"

"We don't use addresses." Cigarette lady had over-plucked her brows to the point she couldn't raise them at me, though from the lines that emerged on her forehead, I was sure she was trying. "I'm sure there's a parcel number, but I don't have it. If you've got a map, we can look it up."

She stood rooted to the floor until Dan leaned onto the counter and flashed her a smile. "We're sorry to be so much trouble, miss, but we'd sure appreciate if you could help us out."

Miss? Cigarette lady was fifty if she was a day. Strike three for her, because she actually blushed. Then she shuffled through a cabinet and found a surveyor's map of the town, pointedly unrolling it in front of Dan. He pointed out the Tilamu property and she jotted down the parcel number, re-rolling the map before I could see it and disappearing into the adjoining room.

I glared at Dan. "Do you want to know or do you want to be right?"

Cigarette lady shuffled back, file in hand. She put the file on the counter, again pointedly addressing only Dan, and told him to let her know if she could do anything else for him. There were things I wanted to say, but I knew I would need a copy of the file so I couldn't afford to antagonize her any more than my existence already had. Dan thanked her and slid the folder to me.

It wasn't very thick. Doc Tilamu had claimed the land when he came back from med school in the late 1950's, before Alaska became a state. Back then, property ownership had been on a handshake basis. People picked out a pretty piece of land, built a house on it and as long as the feds didn't own it, everybody agreed you did. Eventually, the tax assessor would come around, draw up some paperwork and tell you what you owed. Homesteading, long gone in the lower forty-eight, wasn't repealed in Alaska until 1986. By the time the town incorporated and the state's surveyor came around, Doc had lived in the little house for more than ten years.

The state had issued the original deed to the land. There was a copy of Mrs. Tilamu's death certificate in the file and a revised deed removing her name and listing Doc as the sole owner. It was the next piece of paper in the file that floored me. Two years after the death of his wife and a year after the death of her husband, Doc Tilamu had transferred ownership of his property to *Angela K. Nash, widow.*

***

"Why would he do it, Dan?" We were sitting at a table in the hotel's deserted breakfast area. We'd tried sitting on the bed in my room but that had proven uncomfortable so we'd retreated downstairs to the "always hot" coffee pot. "Why would Doc give his house to Mrs. Nash?"

"We don't know that he gave it to her. Maybe he sold it."

"Fine, why would he do that?"

"Maybe he needed money and was too proud to take out a loan."

"Doc was certainly proud, but I can't imagine why he'd need money. Besides, whether he gave it to her or she bought it, why wouldn't she say something after he died?"

"For that matter, why do his children think the house is theirs?" Dan countered. "Wouldn't it have gone through probate after their dad died, just like it's going through probate now?"

"You'd think so. All I know is they asked me to rent it out until they decided what to do about it. Every year, Mrs. Nash asked to rent it and no matter how bad it got, she told me she didn't want to stay anywhere else."

"That's another crazy thing. She obviously knew the house was hers so why would she pay rent to live there?" We'd gone from the land office to the tax office and verified that Mrs. Nash had faithfully paid the property taxes on the little house every year since the land transfer.

"I have no idea." I stared at my cup. The coffee tasted like it had been on the burner all day and there wasn't enough cream in the dispenser to cut through the mud. "Maybe she felt that by paying rent to his kids, she was... I don't know, taking care of them for him."

"What about her own kids?"

"I guess we'll have to wait and hear what Olivia Jordan has to say."

Chapter 5

We were up early the next morning and I was thankful to find the coffee much improved over the previous day's brew. Dr. Jordan was due in at ten-thirty so we ate a quick breakfast and hit the used bookstore. Dan picked out a few books, then stood by the register watching me clean out the mystery section. "Clean out" was perhaps a tad strong. There were books I didn't buy because I'd already read them and, of course, there were those I already had on my e-reader at home but I did leave the section looking a little more bare than I'd found it.

"There is more than one genre to choose from, you know," Dan said as I piled my treasures onto the counter.

"I got a few comedies."

"And a handful of romantic suspense," the shop keeper added as she sorted through the pile, writing prices on a yellow pad.

"There, you see? I'm a multi-faceted connoisseur."

"$26.50," said the woman, looking up from her calculator.

"Let me get that for you."

"I don't wanna share." I handed the woman most of the cash I had with me and said a mental thank you to my father, who'd had the foresight to open a charge account at the marina so we'd never be without gas for the boat on the way home. "You can carry the bags though." I threw my backpack over my shoulder and grabbed Dan's overnight bag, confident his load was quite a bit heavier than mine.

"Let's drop all this at the boat before we head out to the airport." Since cabs are never where you want them when you want them, we walked back to the hotel and had the concierge call one. I waited in the cab while Dan took our things to the boat. When he got back, he was breathing hard and the cab set off for the airport north of town.

"You run pretty well for an old man," I teased. "Don't have a heart attack though, my CPR card expired."

If he'd had any air in his lungs, he might have said something. Instead, he caught my hand and tucked my arm under his. "How are we going to know her?" he asked when he could speak.

"I hadn't thought about it. There can't be that many people on the plane."

"So your plan is to stand at the baggage claim looking for someone who seems to be looking for us?"

"It sounds bad when you say it like that."

"Make it sound better."

"She's supposed to call me when she lands."

"Now that sounds like a plan."

Fifteen minutes later, we were standing in the baggage claim, looking for someone but no one seemed to be looking for us. "Do you see her?" asked Dan.

"Nope."

"Are you sure her plane landed?"

"That's what the sign says."

"Why hasn't she called you?"

I was pacing up and down the baggage area, scanning the faces of the passengers who were straggling by to claim their luggage. Dan was leaning against a post, hands in his jeans pockets, annoyingly calm. I walked up to him. "I have no idea."

"Did you check your phone? Maybe she sent you a text instead."

I pulled the phone out of my pocket. "Nothing."

Dan put his face next to mine and I felt his breath on the back of my neck. "Why don't you call her?"

I thumbed through my received calls until I found the one from Minnesota. "Dr. Jordan? It's Caribou King. We're at baggage claim."

"I'm sorry I'm so slow. I had to take a detour when I got off the plane."

"No problem. I was just hoping we hadn't missed you."

"I'm just walking in. Where are you?"

"Tall, skinny redhead standing by a pole."

"Next to the cute older guy in the leather jacket?"

"That's us. Where are you?"

I heard her voice coming from off to the side as well as from the phone. "Right here."

We turned. A short, dark-haired woman who looked to be in her late twenties or early thirties, casually but smartly dressed, was smiling and waving at us, but there was something Mrs. Nash's attorney hadn't told us about this granddaughter and I almost dropped my phone. Dan put out a hand to steady me and I thought I recovered quickly, or at least I hoped so. I strode forward, extending my hand. "Welcome to Alaska, Dr. Jordan."

She grinned, pushing aside my hand and giving me a hug. "I'm a hugger. I hope it's all right. I feel like I know you, as much as my grandmother talked about you and your family."

"I'm so sorry for your loss. We loved having your grandmother with us every summer, and your grandfather when he was still alive."

A shadow passed across her face, but only briefly. "It's incredibly sad losing Gram like this." She reached out a hand to Dan, without letting go of my waist. "I'm sorry. I didn't mean to leave you out."

"Dr. Jordan, this is my friend, Dan Simmons."

"Olivia, please. I'm still getting used to the doctor part. You'd think after four years of med school and two years of residency, I'd stop looking around to see who they're talking to when somebody asks for Dr. Jordan."

Dan took a step toward the belt, where luggage had begun trundling by. "If you'll tell me what to look for, I'll grab your bags."

She handed him her claim ticket. "It's a soft-sided purple bag with red yarn tied on the handle." She turned back to me as he went off to look for it. "Everybody in Minneapolis has a purple suitcase. I didn't even think about it until I got off the plane the first time. I swear, the whole town's a Vikings fan."

"You must be too."

She shook her head. "I didn't know a thing about football. I learned in self-defense." She studied my face. "My grandmother never told you my father was black, did she?"

I let out a breath I hadn't even realized I'd been holding. "I'm so sorry. You must think I'm a horrible person."

"Prejudice runs deep, but what matters is whether we act on it." She squeezed my hand. "Let's put it on the shelf until we know each other better. It won't spoil for sittin' a spell. That's what my mama used to say and she was almost always right."

"Is your mother from the South?"

"She moved to Tennessee when she got married. She lived there for thirty-three years until cancer took her."

"I'm so sorry."

"I'm just about used to it now."

Dan rejoined us, carrying a violently purple suitcase, and we went to find a cab to take us back to the marina. "Have you been to Alaska before, Dr. Jordan?"

"Call me Olivia, please. I've never had the pleasure, though the way Gram talked, it sounded like heaven."

"You won't get any argument from me. I've lived here all my life and I've never wanted to be anyplace else."

"It's a bit grim today," I said, nodding at the clouds that had once again swallowed the mountain, "but we should have calm seas for the trip home."

"How far is Coho Bay?"

"A few hours."

"And we're going by boat?"

"We have to. You can't drive to Coho Bay. You can't drive to Juneau either, for that matter. We're on an island, though it's so big you'd never know it unless you were looking at a map."

She sat back and looked out at the city. The road from the airport skirted the Mendenhall Wetlands on one side and a residential area on the other. We passed a hospital and a salmon hatchery and Olivia commented on the lack of chain stores.

"We have them," I assured her. "Up along Lemon Creek and back east of the airport, but we like our Mom and Pop's."

"How big is Juneau?"

"Tiny compared to Minneapolis. We don't have as many people in the whole state as you do in your city."

"I wasn't complaining. I was thinking how nice it would be to work in an emergency room where every other case isn't a gunshot wound."

Dan laughed. "We have our share of those, but it's usually 'cuz some idiot got drunk and put a load of buckshot in his buddy's rear end."

"Dan speaks from experience," I said. When she started to laugh I added, "Not because he's been on the wrong end of a shotgun. He's our one and only policeman so he gets all kinds of crazy calls."

"Oh, I get it. There isn't much crime to keep you busy, I'd guess."

"Thank God. We see some shoplifting in the summer and get the odd pick-pocket or break-in, but mostly it's hunting for lost hikers and responding to accidents of one kind or another."

The cab pulled up at the marina and we headed for the boat. Dan cast off and we stopped at the gas pump to fill up. One thing you don't want to do is run out of gas in the middle of nowhere, especially in winter when a storm can blow up at a moment's notice. Once we got out on open water, I throttled up and settled back in the pilot's seat for the trip home.

"Mrs. Nash was your mother's mother?" I had to shout a bit to be heard over the motor.

"Yes, although I didn't know her until a few years ago."

"Really? Why is that?"

"While she was away at college, my mother fell in love with a black man. When she told my grandfather she was going to marry him, she says he hit the roof."

"Just because he was black?"

"It was the 1970's and you didn't see too many inter-racial couples outside of TV. My mother told me he threatened to disown her if she didn't break it off."

"That's crazy."

"Isn't it? I can't imagine somebody doing that now, but he was true to his word. My mother said he never spoke to her from the day she got married to the day he died. My dad was killed in an accident on his job, when I was just a little girl, but even then he wouldn't take her call."

"What about your grandmother?"

"I guess she must've gone along with him. I never had any contact until my mother died."

"You've had a lot of loss for someone so young."

She looked out at the water. The mountains met the waters of the passage in rugged coves and rocky shores. It would have been breathtaking on a clear day, but today the clouds hung low, shutting off the view. We passed a ferry headed north, but otherwise we were alone. "That was three years ago. Mama kept her cancer from me all through med school, but on my last break before I graduated, she was so thin and pale, she had to tell me." She shuddered. "I called the hospital where I had been accepted for my residency and put it off. After she died, I found letters my grandmother had written after my grandfather died. She wanted so much to see us, to make amends. My mother never answered them, but by Gram kept writing. I don't know why my mother didn't throw them away."

The water was choppy, and my arms were getting sore. Dan stepped up behind me and put his hand on the wheel. "Why don't you let me take a turn? You two go below and warm up."

I happily relinquished my seat. I ducked into the cabin and threw myself down on the tiny couch, leaving the bench on the other side of the cabin for Olivia. As she shut the hatch, the rain hit. "It might get a bit rough," I warned her. "If you start to feel green, we can go back up. You get wet, but fresh air is the best cure for seasickness."

"I haven't spent much time on the water," she said, gripping the rail that ran along the wall beside her as the boat lurched. "I've done a little kayaking on the river, but I never seem to have any time. I'm okay so far."

"Before we get to Coho Bay, I should warn you about my mother."

"What about her?"

"She's on a crusade to get a doctor. The minute she heard about you, she started mapping out a plan to get you to stay."

Olivia laughed. "Thanks for the heads-up. You don't already have a doctor?"

"Not since Doc Tilamu died."

"Tilamu? Isn't that the name of Gram's house?"

"One and the same."

"Gram never talked about the house except to say it was a little rustic."

"Truthfully, until her attorney called, we all thought Doc Tilamu's kids inherited it. Mrs. Nash has been paying them rent. I was hoping you could tell me why."

The boat shook violently and she grabbed the rail again. "Gram and I had very little time together. We talked two or three times a month, but I've been working seventy hours a week. By the time I'd get home, all I wanted to do was sleep."

"I don't know how doctors do that. I'd be asleep on my feet."

"There were days I probably was," she admitted, "but every night, I'd cross another day off the calendar and know I was that much closer to being a doctor. Sometimes, that was the only thing that kept me going."

"What are you going to do when you finish?"

"I don't know. I was planning to move to Arizona. Gram was the only family I had."

"What about your father's family?"

"They weren't much happier about the marriage than Mom's. They didn't disown us, but after my dad died, they just stopped coming around."

"That's sad."

She shrugged. "I guess so. I've never had time to chase after people who weren't interested in me. I wouldn't have gone looking for Gram if I hadn't found her letters."

"Maybe that's why your mother saved them."

"Maybe."

"You look tired. Was it a bad flight?"

She ran her hand through her hair. "I've been fighting just to stay upright. Gram..." She gulped, brushing a tear from her face. "We had such plans. I was going to take the next summer off. We were going to come up here together and... She said the place could use some fixing."

Her pain was so raw, it didn't seem like the time to tell her just how much fixing the house needed. I listened to the thrum of the engine, letting the movement of the boat lull me to sleep. The change in the intensity woke me some time later, but I was alone in the cabin. I pushed myself off the couch and followed the sound of laughter onto the deck.

Olivia was perched on the captain's seat, steering the boat, her hair tied back and her eyes bright. "Hello, sleepyhead," she greeted me as I climbed out of the cabin. "Dan told me about your bout with pneumonia. I thought we'd better let you sleep."

"I'm fine." A yawn betrayed me.

"You were right about the seasickness. Went away the minute I took hold of the wheel."

"You look like you're enjoying yourself."

"If I'd known it was this much fun to drive a boat, I'd have tried it years ago."

Dan got up from the passenger seat, offering it to me. I smiled and slid into it, while he stood behind me. "You forget the fun part of it. Up here, it's just something we do to get from one place to another."

"Speak for yourself," I told him. "I loved taking Dad's boat out on Thursdays, until the motor kept conking out on me and I'd have to row my way home."

"That boat must've been older than you are."

"Oh, easily."

"I thought this was your boat," said Olivia. "The Sea Pallet, right? Sounds like an art dealer's boat."

"It does, doesn't it? It belonged to my friend Johnny, who was a painter. His dad gave it to me after Johnny died because he know our boat was dead in the water."

"I'm sorry to hear about your friend."

"Everybody has losses to cope with." I looked around for landmarks.

"We'll be at the mouth of the bay in twenty minutes or so," said Dan.

I nodded, watching Olivia. The tiredness had dropped away and she had lost ten years from her face. How sad that she was coming to Coho Bay to bury her grandmother, instead of spending the summer relaxing, exploring and getting to know each other. Why would Mrs. Nash kill herself when she was so close to repairing the damage done forty years ago? It didn't make any sense. I looked at Dan and wondered if his thoughts echoed mine.

"I should take over from here," I said. "The entrance to the bay is trickier than it looks."

We traded seats. "Where do the cruise ships dock?"

"The marina isn't deep enough so they anchor in the middle of the bay, where it's not only deep but wide enough for them to turn around. You can't believe how little space those great big ships need to spin around in. They shuttle passengers in on tenders—lifeboats," I added when she looked puzzled.

I steered around a large rock formation and turned into the bay. It was late afternoon and the sun had already sunk below the horizon, leaving a dusky remnant just bright enough to see if you knew what you were looking at. I flipped on the boat's cruising lights and watched lights flicker on here and there on shore, in greater number as we came closer to town.

"It's enchanting," breathed Olivia, just barely loud enough for me to hear her over the motor. "Like a fairy city."

Dan snickered. "It's pretty," I offered, thinking it looked the same to me as it always did.

Olivia smiled at us. "You two are spoiled, growing up with all this. I grew up in Memphis. It's pretty enough, but it's nothing like this."

"You had Elvis," I said, cutting back the motor.

"He died before I was ever a twinkle in my mother's eyes."

I tried to look at my hometown through the eyes of someone seeing it for the first time, but it was too familiar. There were too many ghosts of myself and my sister, my friends and my parents, everywhere I looked. "I guess you never quite see home the way someone coming in from the outside does."

"Can you see the house from here? Gram said it has a beautiful view of the bay."

"You could if there was enough daylight." I pointed at the homes on the far side of the water. I could just make out the outline of the house against the shore, but I doubted Olivia would be able to pick it out. "We'll head over in the morning. Your grandmother was being charitable with her assessment of how much work it needs. I'm afraid no one's put any money into it since Doc died."

"Could I see her?"

I looked at Dan before answering. "Kenny would have taken her to the church, wouldn't he?"

"Let Cara get you settled in first and I'll check on that. Where are you putting her?"

"I could stay at Gram's house."

"No, you wouldn't want to do that. You can stay in my apartment."

"I wouldn't want to put you out."

"It's no trouble. I can bunk at my sister's place while you're in town."

I eased the boat into the berth we'd vacated the day before and Dan jumped out to tie off. Olivia helped me button up the boat cover while he went ahead to drop off her suitcase and check on the church. We walked up the dock and climbed the steps to the wooden boardwalk. "That's my gallery," I said. "The apartment is upstairs. We'll head over to Mel's first though. They'll be holding dinner for us."

"It's a beautiful building."

"Thank you. My dad and I swing a mean hammer, if I don't say so myself."

"You built it yourself?"

"You pretty much have to out here. We have a lumber mill, and there's a terrific carpenter who makes cabinets and furniture, but a contractor would starve to death in Coho Bay."

She shook her head. "It's a whole other world."

"I don't have much experience to go by, but I'm with Dan. I wouldn't want to live anyplace else."

"Your husband's a nice guy. I don't remember Gram mentioning you were married."

"Dan? He's not my... We're just... What gave you that idea?"

"I'm sorry. I didn't mean to embarrass you."

"No. It's just, we only started... I don't think you could call it dating even. It's not like there's anywhere to go."

Olivia chuckled. "Hit a nerve, didn't I? It's the way he looks at you, the way you act together. Like you fit."

"We've known each other for years, that's all."

"Is Dan from Coho Bay too?"

"He was born and raised in Homer, then worked in Fairbanks, but he spent his summers here growing up, then his vacations once he was out of school."

We'd reached Mel's by then, and swung around the building to the kitchen entrance since I knew the restaurant would be locked. I knocked, then opened the door, "I'm back, with company!"

"We're up here, Caribou."

I turned to Olivia. "That's my mother. Remember—"

"Twisting my arm to stay. Gotcha."

I led her up the stairs and into what was the new family room. "You guys are amazing! It looks finished."

"We saved some work for you," my dad told me and I threw my arms around him.

"I can't believe how much you got done while I was gone."

"Frank was a big help," he said, nodding his head toward the window, where Frank was leaning against the wall.

"Caribou, where are your manners? Aren't you going to introduce us?" Without waiting for me, Mom strode across the room and pulled Olivia into the room. "You must be Dr. Jordan. I'm Marcia King, Caribou's mother. This is my husband, Robert, my other daughter, Melody and her husband Bentley Andrews." She indicated each person in turn.

"Call me Bent," said my brother-in-law, who hated his given name. Olivia gave each of them a welcoming hug, asking Mel when her baby was due.

"In February," she answered, stroking the barely-there bump. "Welcome to Coho Bay, Dr. Jordan."

"It's Olivia, please."

Mel smiled. "Olivia."

Mom gestured toward Frank. "And this is Caribou's young man, Franklin Baker."

Olivia looked at me, her expression puzzled, but she walked over to greet Frank while I shot a death glare at my mother. Frank grinned at me and returned Olivia's hug. "Glad to meet you. I gotta say, though. You aren't what I was expecting."

"Frank!" I said.

Olivia waved me off. "It's okay, Cara." She turned back to Frank. "My grandmother must not have told anyone that my father was African-American."

"Well, that too, but I was talkin' about you bein' so young and pretty."

Olivia laughed and turned back to me. "This Frank of yours is quite a charmer."

"He's not my Frank," I said, then regretted my bluntness when I saw the hurt on Frank's face. "I'm sorry, I didn't mean it like that. It's just..."

"Why don't we go and get dinner ready, Bent?" Mel offered and I shot her a grateful look.

"You stay put, honey-bunch," said Dad. "Bent and I can manage."

"Or we could all go down and eat in the dining room, Robert. We don't have a table up here for family meals." Mom took Olivia's arm. "Dr. Jordan, I want to talk to you about your future. Have you considered going into practice in a small but vibrant town that is rapidly becoming an art mecca and a tourist destination?"

Olivia winked at me and went with her. The rest of my family followed them and I waited for them to disappear down the stairs. "Frank, I'm sorry. I didn't mean to hurt your feelings."

He put his arms around me and drew me into a more than friendly hug. "You could never hurt my feelings, Boo."

The pet name grated, but I shoved that aside. "My mother—"

"Is just blowin' smoke. Don't you let it bother you."

He leaned down and kissed me, long and slow and dizzyingly sensual. My heart raced, my mind swirled and my body melted against his. His body was asking for something I knew I wasn't ready to deliver so I pulled away, gasping for air. I couldn't meet his eyes as I turned away, almost tripping on my own feet. "We'd better not keep them waiting," I managed to get out as I fled for the safety of the kitchen.

My mother gave me a long look, head to toe, as I came into the dining room, but she said nothing. I took a seat next to Olivia, and Frank joined us, thankfully sitting across the table. I didn't trust myself to have my thigh pressed against him or my knees bumping up against his. Olivia was deep in conversation with Mel so I helped myself to a filet of salmon and even took a serving of unidentifiable greens my mother must have made. Bent's salmon usually melts in your mouth, a delicious combination of sweet and savory only he knows the secret to, but tonight I might have been eating sawdust.

There was a knock on the street door and my dad went to open it for Dan, who stomped the snow off his boots before joining us. "Daniel," said my mother, her hand on an empty chair at her end of the table, "won't you join us?"

Dan pulled a chair from an adjoining table and placed himself between me and Frank, who was looking none too happy to see him. "Thank you, Marcie, Bent's cooking sure beats anything I've got waiting for me at home."

"Try the greens," I said, handing him the bowl.

"They're dandelion," explained my mother. I hoped my face didn't have the same expression as Dan's, but I was pretty sure it did. "They're very high in vitamin K."

"What the heck is vitamin K?" whispered Dan and I shrugged.

"Purifies the blood," said Frank, scooping up a forkful and managing to eat it with only a slight change in his expression.

"They're also a wonderful source of vitamins A and C," added Olivia, who was eating hers as though she actually enjoyed them. "These are wonderfully done, Marcie."

I took a hesitant bite but the acrid taste overcame my manners and I spit it out. Olivia laughed. "It's an acquired taste. Do you grow your own, Marcie?"

"I'd love to have a garden, but I never seem to have time. Winter's my only down season. The rest of the year, I'm busy as a bee keeping up with my work."

"What kind of work do you do?"

My mother beamed and launched into a detailed explanation of her duties as a wildlife biologist. "Robert also works for the state," she said, finally reaching the end of her narrative. "When I got the opportunity to work in Alaska, we were afraid he would have difficulty finding work but environmental science is very much in demand here, as are medical professionals."

"See how she managed to slide that in?" I asked.

Olivia nodded. "She's good."

"Excuse me?" asked my mother.

"I warned Olivia you'd be all over her trying to get her to move to Coho Bay."

"It's fine, Marcie, really. I'm flattered." Olivia declined the slice of pie Mel offered and pushed back her chair. "I hate to break up what's been an enjoyable evening, but I would like to see my grandmother and then I think it's time to hit the hay."

"Don't say that too loud." Frank also pushed back his chair, "They'll have you sleeping on a bale in the woodshed."

"Now Franklin, Robert and I use those cots every year when we do the moose count. They are perfectly adequate and the kitchen is hardly a woodshed."

"Moose count?"

"I'll explain it to you later, Olivia." I stood up, wondering why Frank was sleeping on a cot in Mel's kitchen but not wanting to stick around to find out. "I'll take you over to the church and then get you settled in the apartment. Mom, I'm going to sleep on the couch over there tonight."

"As you wish," said Mom. Frank shot me a look that was, I'm not sure. Disappointment? Frustration? Perhaps a bit of both.

"I'll go with you," said Dan, popping the last of his pie into his mouth. "I'll need to unlock the church for you."

He and Frank stood eying each other, reminding me of two bull elk during rut. "Why don't you give me the key?" I asked, holding out my hand. "We ladies can get along just fine on our own."

Frank glared at me, but sat back down and Mel handed him a large slice of pie. Dan dug the key out of his pocket and handed it to me. "I'll walk over with you. It's on my way home."

"Daniel, my daughter is quite capable of showing the good doctor to the church. Robert was hoping to show you the progress we've made on the remodel project."

Olivia and I grabbed our coats and slipped out the back, leaving Dad's discussion of the virtues of raw cut lumber behind us. We crossed the empty street and past the bank. We turned onto Second Street and started up the wooden sidewalk. As we walked past the recreation hall, I pointed it out to Olivia. "The ladies guilds will be hosting a gathering here after the interment."

"That's so kind of them. I hate to put people to so much trouble, and on short notice."

"It's no trouble. Your grandmother was part of life here and everyone wanted to do something to help."

Olivia didn't speak right away and when she did, there was a break in her voice. "I love these wooden sidewalks."

"The tourists love them too, which is how we got the mayor to lay out the money for them, but as it turns out, they're also more practical than cement sidewalks would have been."

"They have personality."

I laughed. "We have loads of personality here. Not always a good thing."

"I noticed. You seem to have two handsome men fighting over you."

I was thankful for the fading light so she didn't see the flush come over my cheeks. "We're not exactly overflowing with single women, that's all."

"I'm sure it has nothing to do with those gorgeous green eyes of yours."

"Don't be silly. Mel's the beauty of the family. Especially right now."

"Your sister is lovely, but you have a strength that men find very attractive. Strong men are looking for strong women."

"Did your mother always say that?"

"As a matter of fact, she did. Whenever I complained that every man I went out with couldn't handle my determination to become a doctor."

"I think your mom would have liked mine."

"I'm sure she would have. Marcie reminds me of her. You're lucky to have her."

I didn't feel lucky when Mom was trying to run my life, but if I'd lost her as Olivia had lost her mother, I knew I'd be devastated. "Here's the church." I unlocked the door while Olivia read the sign beside it.

"Three different churches in one building?" she asked.

"It was originally Russian Orthodox, but nobody saw the need for more buildings, so we all share."

"Very thrifty."

"Saved money, but time is as precious a commodity to us. We're not busy in the winter, but it's too cold to build. Once it gets warm enough, everybody's working ten or twelve hours a day. We have the tourist trade, of course, but we also have a thriving cannery. The fishing boats go out every day before dawn and when they get back, they have to process the catch."

"That's hard work, I'd guess."

"And dangerous too. We really do need a doctor. If somebody gets seriously hurt, having on-site treatment could be the difference between life and death."

"Your mom said you have a clinic."

"Yes, we walked past it on the way here. I'll give you a tour of it in the morning if you want. Not that I'm trying to pressure you or anything."

She laughed. "I would like to see it. I finish my residency in the spring but after that, I'm at a loss where I should go. Gram hinted there might be a place for me here. Her attorney is advising me to sell, but Gram would have hated that. If nothing else, I plan to keep it as a vacation home."

We hung our coats on a rack in the entry and walked into the sanctuary. The overhead lighting seemed harsh with just the two of us. "I have always loved this room," I said, my voice hushed for no good reason. "As long as I can remember, we've come to church every Sunday, rotating times with the two other congregations. I've seen it in all times of the day and night."

"It's beautiful," she whispered, looking around her. There were stained glass windows that sparkled in the morning sunshine but looked dull against the darkness outside. Rows of pews with red upholstered cushions flanked a center aisle leading to the altar. An orthodox cross, covered in gold-leaf, stood behind the altar, pictures of Mary, Jesus and the apostles decorating the far wall.

Mrs. Nash's coffin sat on a table in front of the altar. I sat in one of the pews and let Olivia go to her grandmother alone. Someone had carved Mrs. Nash's name on the top of the coffin and she reached out and ran her fingers over the letters. She tried to open the lid, but the same person who had done the carving must have had the foresight to seal it. Still trying to blot out the last time I'd seen Mrs. Nash, I said a silent prayer of thanks for that bit of thoughtfulness.

"Why did you do it?" Olivia's voice was low, but since there was no other sound I could easily hear what she was saying. I shifted uncomfortably, feeling as though I was intruding. She turned, reaching out her hand to me and I stepped forward to grasp it. Her face was stricken, tears flowing unchecked. "Why would you leave me like this, Gram?"

I gathered her in my arms as she sobbed. Nothing I could say could blunt that pain so I stayed quiet, letting her grieve. I couldn't imagine how it would feel to lose everyone I loved and know that I was unwelcome by the only family I had left. Olivia was truly alone and her shoulders seemed painfully slim to carry such weight.

Chapter 6

Olivia was still sleeping when I woke at dawn the next morning. Knowing how emotionally draining the visit to the church had been, I decided to let her sleep. I scribbled a note for her to meet me at Mel's when she got up and slipped out. The sun was still rising over the mountains and I stopped to watch. The scattered clouds were stained pink and gold. The mountains were white, with the dark green of the evergreens running up to the line where the trees gave way to barren, rugged peaks. The air was biting and I pulled my stocking cap lower to cover my ears.

Nature enveloped me, permeating the air I breathed, penetrating the very core of my being until I was part of the environment and it was part of me. During the year I'd spent at school in Seattle, it was the ground and the water and the sky I missed as much as my family and friends. Seattle is a beautiful city, but I was born and bred for this tiny Alaskan village.

"It's really something, isn't it?"

I jumped. "Frank, you've gotta stop sneaking up on me."

"I'm not sneaking. I was headed to Mel's for breakfast."

I looked behind him. "Where are you headed from? I thought you were sleeping in the kitchen?"

"I bunked down in my boat last night." He turned me back to the sunrise, which had progressed from pinks and golds to bright white against the blue sky. He put his arms around me and whispered, "Could have used a bunkmate to keep me warm."

A slow heat spread through me. "You're moving too fast, Frank."

"Tell me you don't like this." His lips brushed against my neck as his hands moved down my arms, pulling me closer. Every inch of my body was screaming for me to let go of my fears and explore sensations that were driving my heart rate higher than the every other Wednesday aerobic dance class at the recreation center.

I turned to face him. "You're a good looking man, Frank. It's obvious I'm attracted to you."

"Then what are we waiting for?" He tugged my hand and took a step toward the dock. "Let's take the boat out. We'll anchor at a quiet cove and see where this thing takes us."

I planted my feet. "I can't do that."

He swept me into his arms and kissed me, pulling my hips against his. I managed to break off the kiss before it got too far out of control. He took my face in his hands. "Tell me you don't want this and I'll walk away."

"I like you and I'd like to get to know you better, but I don't jump into bed with a man because I'm attracted to him, Frank. Sex means something to me and I don't have any idea what it means to you, or whether it means the same thing or if it means anything at all."

"Why does it have to mean anything?" He caught my hands. "Why does it have to mean anything other than I want to be with you and you want to be with me?"

"Right now." He looked puzzled. "You want to be with me right now and I want to be with you right now too, but 'right now' isn't a good enough reason."

He took a step back. "Cara, are you a virgin?"

My face flared red, but so did my temper. "If I go with you, I'm sure it would be incredible but I'm gonna start feeling things for you that I'm not ready to feel. I'm gonna start wanting things from you that I don't think you're ready to give."

Frank's eyes went cold and I sensed a wall going up between us. "It's too fast, Frank. If you're only interested in sex, no harm, no foul, but I'm not the one for you. If you're genuinely interested in me, then let's slow down and take time to get to know each other."

He stared at me for a long moment and I found myself holding my breath until he sighed and put his arm around my shoulder. "Let's eat. I don't know about you, but I'm starving to death."

I put my arm around his waist and matched his pace as we turned toward Mel's. I still didn't like the idea of being caught between two men, but at least now maybe I'd get to see the real Frank and not the romance cover model he'd been showing me.

***

Mel hadn't come down for breakfast, but the frittatas Bent had whipped up were every bit as good as the ones she made once a week during the season. He'd opened the restaurant to accommodate the people who would be in town for the funeral over the next couple of days. There were a few tables already occupied and Dad was serving coffee, white apron tied around his waist. I kissed him on the cheek and offered to set him free.

"Have your breakfast first. I see you've found Frank."

"He slept in his boat."

"I wasn't insinuating anything, honey. I don't care what your mother says, those cots are worse than sleeping on the floor."

Olivia came in as Frank and I were finishing breakfast so I pushed him and Dad to go upstairs while

I went to work waiting tables. "We should be able to finish your room today," Dad told me as they headed up, "so you won't have to camp out on your couch."

"I still don't have a bed."

"There's always a cot." He smiled and avoided the dishtowel I threw at him.

"We can take the sleds out when we get done and haul in the furniture from your cabin," offered Bent, as he scrambled eggs to fill an order.

"You have a cabin?" asked Olivia.

"About five miles out. If you're up for it, you can ride out with us this afternoon. It'll be cold."

"I can loan her my snowmobile suit," said Mel, who had come down to the kitchen to get orange juice.

"Perfect! Bent, this frittata is amazing. You could make a killing if you had a place in Minneapolis."

My sister smiled and her hand instinctively went to her baby bump. "But then we'd have to live there."

She and the guys went upstairs and I poured Olivia a cup of coffee, keeping an eye on the tables with guests. "What all would you like to do today, Olivia?"

"When is the funeral?"

"Tomorrow morning. We would have held it this afternoon, but they had to get the grave ready."

"Permafrost?"

"Not this far south, but that's a good guess. The ground they picked a billion years ago for the cemetery is the rockiest place on the bay. They have to haul out the heavy equipment."

"I should make arrangements to cover the costs."

"I think Mr. Clarke has taken care of that already, but we can stop by City Hall to double check."

"Sounds good. I also want to take a look at the clinic and go over the house to see how much work it will need."

The bell on the front door chimed as Dan came in. I went into the kitchen to make up a plate for him but Bent shooed me out. "I know what your boyfriend wants, little sister."

"He's not my boyfriend."

I went back into the dining room. "Morning, Dan. I see you've got your coffee." He held his mug up to salute me and I set a plate of frittata and diner fries in front of him. I pulled the church key from my pocket and tossed it to him.

"Everything look okay for the service?" he asked Olivia.

She frowned. "I understand the coffin being closed for the funeral, but I wanted to see Gram. It's hard to say goodbye to a pine box."

"Did your attorney tell you how Mrs. Nash died?" asked Dan. "It's not pretty."

"I'm a doctor. I'm just finishing my rotation in the emergency room of a major metropolitan area. I assure you, I've seen some pretty horrific things."

"It's not the same when it's family."

"Why don't we start with the house?" I suggested. "I haven't had a chance to clean up the living room. If seeing that doesn't bother you, I'm sure we can unseal the coffin and give you time alone with your grandmother."

"Give me a call when you know and I can head over there and take care of that for you."

"That sounds fine." Olivia put her fork down. "That was the best breakfast I've had in years."

"You've probably been eating most of your meals in a hospital cafeteria," I said, getting up to bus the table. "Dan, you want anything else while I'm in the kitchen?"

"Nope, just leave the coffee pot on."

I turned to the other diners, "I'm heading out. Anyone need anything before I go?" No one did, so I went into the kitchen and put the dirty dishes in the dishwasher. Bent had finished the order he'd been working on and I reached for it. Mel was sitting on a stool, watching him wash dishes. "Olivia and I are going to take a look at the Tilamu house, then head over so she can see the clinic. Want to come?"

Mel looked uncertain. "I still have so much to do."

"Like what? There's hardly anybody here and Dan can look after himself. It'd do you good to get out in the fresh air. Besides," I lowered my voice, "Olivia's thinking about moving to Coho Bay and I'd rather have you than Mom helping me tilt her in our direction."

"Well, when you put it that way." Mel beamed at me and hopped off the stool. "Bent, I'll be with Cara if you need me."

"Okay, hon. Have fun."

"You two look like you're up to something," Dan commented.

"Just getting some fresh air," I said, dropping the plate of eggs off for the person who'd ordered them. "I'll call you when we need you."

"Oh, it feels wonderful to be outside again," said Mel as we hit the boardwalk. She threw out her arms and spun around. "Just smell that air."

"We don't let her out very often," I said to Olivia. Mel gave me a playful shove and we set off up the boardwalk.

"I'd like to know the history of the house," said Olivia. "Gram didn't tell me very much."

"Doc Tilamu built it for his wife when he got back from med school."

"Doc was a local?

"Born and raised," said Mel. "So was Mrs. T. They got married while he was still in school because they couldn't bear to be parted after him being away so long during the war. That's when they met your grandparents. Doc went to school with your grandfather."

"Did they help build the house?"

"They didn't start coming out until Doc's kids had grown up and gone. Isn't that right, Mel?"

"Yep. Doc had three children, two girls and a boy. They were restless to see the world and once they left Coho Bay, they never came back."

"That's normal for small towns, isn't it."

"A lot of our kids do move away," I agreed. "Although now that we have the cruise ships, more of them are able to find work here so more are choosing to stay."

"What kind of work?"

"Some opened shops, like I did. Others take cruisers on tours, boat tours and walking tours, fishing. That's what Frank was doing before Jack asked him to take over the lumber mill."

"Sounds like you're a town full of entrepreneurs."

"Stubborn is more like it," laughed Mel. "Nobody wants to take orders from a boss."

"You and Bent run the restaurant all by yourselves?"

"For the most part. At the height of the season— June through August—we bring a college kid in to work for the summer, but otherwise, we're a two person operation. Cara gets art students to come down for the summer to help in the gallery, so sometimes she'll slip away on a really busy day to help me with the lunch rush and she's always there in the morning to help get breakfast started."

"I have to earn all those meals Bent gives me."

"What are you going to do when the baby comes?"

"Make a place for her, or him, in the kitchen. Carry the baby around on one of those slings while I'm waiting tables. I might get more tips that way." She smiled, her thoughts a mile away. "Once he or she starts running around, that's when it'll get complicated. Maybe Cara can watch her for me."

"She'll be better off in the dining room than running around in the gallery. Can you imagine? Knocking over sculptures and putting sticky fingerprints on the paintings?" I shuddered. "I am never having kids."

Olivia laughed at me. "You may feel differently about that someday soon."

"What's that mean?"

"You looked pretty chummy with Frank down by the peer this morning."

"I knew somebody was watching us! I had that creepy-crawly feeling."

"I don't think that was the only feeling you were having."

"Did I miss an ooey-gooey love scene? Sis, you're holding out on me."

We'd reached City Hall and I practically lunged at the door. "C'mon, Olivia. Let's ask Tammy about those funeral costs."

"You can change the subject now, but you are going to tell me everything," said Mel, following me inside.

"Everything about what, girls?" asked Tammy brightly.

I knew better than to put juicy information in front of Tammy. "About Mrs. Nash's funeral expenses, Tammy. This is Dr. Olivia Jordan, her granddaughter."

"Glad to meet you, honey. I'm sorry about your loss."

"Thank you, ma'am. Tammy, is it?"

"Sure thing, and everybody calls me that, so don't you trouble yourself with that ma'am stuff. What would you like to know?"

"I want to settle the costs."

"There's nothing to settle. That nice lawyer fellow in Arizona told me to fax him the bills, 'cause your grandmother pre-paid for everything."

Olivia raised her eyebrows. "When did she do that? Right before she... died?"

"Not at all, sugar. Dan asked me that too. Sometimes somebody comes in here and buys a plot and I tell him, you'd better go check on so and so, cuz it ain't like them to be thinking about the hereafter all of a sudden, but that wasn't your grandma." Tammy reached behind her and pulled a binder off the shelf, thumbing through the pages. Finding the one she wanted, she read from it. "She came in with Doc Tilamu when he was layin' his poor wife to rest. Poor woman suffered so much from the cancer. It was a real blessin' when she died."

"She bought a plot for herself and her husband way back then?" I turned to Olivia. "I wonder why she didn't have him buried here when he died."

"She didn't buy one for him," said Tammy, looking up from the binder. "She said he had a family plot back home, but she weren't too fond of his family. Said she'd rather be laid to rest up here so Doc said to put her next to the place he was gettin' for himself and his wife. That's what we did and that's the spot where they'll be layin' her to rest tomorrow, poor soul."

"Over my dead body." All heads turned to see a middle-aged man, his face flaccid around the edges and his waist bulging over the belt he'd hitched at least one too spots too tight.

There was something familiar about him. "Alexander Tilamu, mind your manners. You got no call to be talking like that to Mrs. Nash's granddaughter. What did you say your name was again, honey?"

"Olivia." She held out her hand to him, but he made no move to take it.

"Dr. Tilamu was my father. He built that house for my mother and for me and my sisters. I'm not letting you steal it from us and I'm sure as hell not letting them bury that witch next to anywhere near my mother."

"That plot is bought and paid for, Alex Tilamu," said Tammy. "You ain't got nothin' to say about it."

"Alex," I said, moving to stand between him and Tammy. He blinked and re-focused his eyes on me. I wondered how much he'd had to drink. "I went to Juneau myself and pulled the land records. Doc transferred title to the property to Mrs. Nash years ago. Nobody knew about it, but I can give you a copy of the records."

"I don't care what the records show. That house is mine!" He stepped around me and put his finger a few inches from Olivia's face. "I'll see you in court." He spun around, losing his balance but he managed to right himself before he fell. Straightening his back, he marched out and headed toward the dock.

"That was pleasant," said Olivia when he'd gone.

"I'm so sorry," I told her, my breath slowly returning to normal after the unpleasant confrontation. "I had no idea Alex was in town."

"Is he always so charming?"

"I don't know. I've never met him. When I've spoken with him on the phone, he's been polite. You must have known him, Tammy."

"He looks like a bad imitation of his daddy at that age. Came busting in here first thing this morning, demanding to talk to Dan. When I told him he wasn't here, he asked for Clem, but he wasn't here either. I told him to come back later. He must have been killing his time in a bottle."

"I'm sorry, Olivia. He was way out of line."

"I had no idea he thought he owned the house. It must have come as quite a shock."

"It was a shock to everybody. Mrs. Nash paid rent for years as though they were the owners and here all along, she was. It doesn't make sense."

Olivia shrugged. "Maybe she felt sorry for them. Gram told me she'd changed her will after I came back into her life. Maybe she had been planning to leave the house to them, but changed her mind. I hate to deprive him and his sisters of something they've been counting on all these years. Maybe I should just give it to them. I have her townhouse in Arizona, after all."

"You're not depriving them of anything," said Mel. "That house is a disaster."

"It's a disaster because they wouldn't pay to maintain it," I pointed out. "Maybe they knew all along the house wasn't theirs and he's just making a big stink about it, hoping to guilt you into giving it back."

"Long way to come for that. How'd he even know she'd be here?" asked Mel.

"He didn't," supplied Tammy. "He was lookin' for Dan, not Doc Olivia."

"Where does he live?" asked Olivia.

"Tacoma," I answered.

"I thought he was in D.C."

"One of his sisters lives in D.C. The older one. I can't remember what she does, it's been so long since I've spoken with her. His other sister lives in Montana, I think. Her husband has something to do with the oil business."

"Tacoma's still a long way just to come just to throw a fit, Cara."

"Well how should I know why Alex does what he does? I don't even know the guy."

"Let's go take a look at the house," said Olivia. "I want to see what he's so upset about."

***

I walked Olivia through the house, showing her the work that absolutely had to be done and pointing out things I thought should be done if she were going to be comfortable there. She'd stood a long time in the living room with its tell-tale stains and we were now standing on the back patio with Mel, who'd decided not to go with us on the tour.

"Tell me how you found her." Olivia's expression was grim, but determined. "I need to know."

I told her, leaving out as much of the gore as I could, trying to remember other details. "I'm sorry, that's as much as I can tell you," I finished. "I was a little freaked out."

"She was screaming like a banshee," said Mel.

"At least I was moving," I countered. "You would have fainted."

"I would not."

"Oh no? You remember that moose carcass we came across in the woods? The one we got away from as fast as we could because it looked like a fresh kill and we didn't want to be dessert?"

"I didn't faint."

"Until we got home."

"Ladies," said Olivia breaking in, "it's nothing to be ashamed of. You should have seen me the first time they brought a GSW into the ER. I bet I was whiter than either one of you."

"I'm sorry," said Mel. "It's very disrespectful of what you're going through."

"Humor makes the heart heal faster," she said. She looked out over the bay. "It's a ton of work, but it might be worth it to have this view."

"I'm working on an appraisal for Mr. Clarke. The real value of this property is the land. I've already had a developer call me asking about it. I don't even know how he knew it might come on the market."

"What would he do with the house?"

"Tear it down and build something bigger, fancier, full of glass and stainless steel," said Mel.

Olivia smiled at her. "Tell me how you really feel, Mel."

"I'm sorry. I have nothing against new and shiny and I suppose if this were my land and I had the money to do it, with no emotional attachment to the house, I'd probably tear it down and start over. It's been neglected too long."

"It's a project, that's for sure." She looked out at the water, where the weekly ferry from Juneau had just pulled up anchor. I hoped Alex was on it. "Could it be made livable in time for me to move in next summer?"

"Are you going to move to Coho Bay?" Mel tried to keep the excitement out of her voice.

"I'd like to have it as a vacation home, if nothing else. I'm afraid I'll miss the arrival of your little one though. I have to finish my residency."

"Well, let's go take a look at the clinic," I suggested, "and trust me, if you decide to move here, my mother will move Heaven and Earth to get the house ready for you in time."

***

We were standing in one of the clinic's empty exam rooms when my phone beeped. "It's Bent," I said. "They're ready to go. Are you interested in riding out to the cabins, Olivia?"

"I'd love to. You know, this clinic is beautiful. What faith your town must have had to build it."

"That's my Mother," explained Mel. "After Doc died, she's been a one woman campaign team, trying to convince the town to attract a new doctor. There are some great incentives between the state and the feds to get student loans reduced or forgiven but she felt if we had a good facility, it would assure a doctor that they wouldn't be going back to the nineteenth century by coming here."

"I wonder that nobody else from the bay has gone to med school over the years," sighed Olivia as we closed up the building and put the key back in the mailbox.

"A few have," I told her, "but so far, once they've gone, they've stayed gone."

"What about your midwife? Would I be stepping on toes with her?"

"Gabby's getting up in years," said Mel.

"She delivered me."

"That alone would make anyone want retire," Mel said, making a face. "I think she'd be happy to have somebody to share the load with, so long as they didn't disrespect what she does."

"I could never do that. Midwives and doulas are a wonderful addition to modern medicine. Their care is so calming for mother and baby, it's better for everyone if I step into a birth only when they need me."

"Then you'll have Gabby's support."

"Will she be at Gram's funeral?"

"The whole town will be there," I said.

"She must have been well loved here," said Olivia.

Mel and I exchanged looks. "Those of us who knew her well will miss her, but Mrs. Nash kept to herself. I'm not sure many people really knew her."

"Then why will the whole town come to her funeral?"

"Because that's what we do."

Back at Mel's, Bent and Frank were pouring gas into the snowmobiles. They had rigged a platform sled between the two that my father and Bent used to haul firewood. "Do you want to come, hon?" asked Bent when Mel walked over to see what he was doing.

"No, I think little Ernie here had better wait awhile before his first sled run."

"Ernie?" I asked, making a face at her.

"Or Penny," answered Bent.

"Please tell me those aren't the real names."

"What's the matter with them?" asked Mel, with a twinkle in her eye.

"You'll never guess who we saw at City Hall," I said, walking over to my mother, who was standing to one side, supervising.

"Alex Tilamu?"

"He came here?"

"With his sister. I barely recognized them. He was such a promising young man. The years have not been kind."

"Alex practically accused Olivia of stealing his house. What'd they want with you?"

"Much the same. And that we'd be hearing from their attorney. Not that they have any grounds for action, considering what you found out about the deed."

"I feel sorry for them," said Olivia, joining us.

"There's nothing for you to feel sorry about," I told her. "Where'd they go? Are they staying in town somewhere?"

"There wasn't anywhere they could stay," Mom replied. "We have no place for them and they certainly couldn't stay at the house. I assume they went back to Juneau with the ferry."

My father came out of Mel's, a high-powered rifle in each hand, which he gave to Bent and Frank. They slid them into slings on the sleds made especially for them.

"Are we expecting trouble?" asked Olivia.

"Not this time of year," he answered, "but it's better safe than sorry."

She looked uncertain, but didn't ask. As my father said, this time of year was pretty quiet but you might still encounter a bear trying to pack on a few more pounds before hibernation. Later in the season, when small game became scarce, you had to be on your guard for wolves, which hunt in packs and had been known to track snowmobiles. You didn't want to be out there alone and break down.

"I'm wondering whether you could help me with something, Mr. King."

"What do you need?"

"Cara and I did a walk-through of the house. It's pretty bad, but I was wondering how long it would take to make the place livable."

"Were you thinking of renting it out next summer?"

"Or living in it yourself, Dr. Jordan?" asked my mother.

"I'm not sure so please don't mention it to anyone. You folks need a doctor and I'll need a place to set up practice. If it's possible to fix it up, and if I could do it on a budget—I know everybody thinks doctors are rich but I'm not. I'm sure that's why Gram left me the house."

"I will have that house looking shipshape by—when did you say you'd be coming?"

"Early June, if it's possible."

"That's gonna be cutting it tight," said my father, running his hand through his hair. "Once the cruise ship season starts, things get a little crazy around here."

"Nonsense, Robert. We'll mobilize the whole town if we have to. I promise you, Dr. Jordan, if you're gracious enough to open a practice here, by June 1 that house will be ready."

***

"Your mother's quite the dynamo," said Olivia as she and I helped Bent and Frank load bedroom furniture onto the sled.

"You don't know the half of it," I told her, "but it's nice to see her using her powers for good. You don't want to see her when she's trying to push you in a direction you don't want to go."

"Heart of gold, hands of steel."

"Exactly. Would you like to see the rest of the place? Mel and Bent's cabin's identical to mine, but my parents' is a little bigger. It has the only kitchen. When we all lived here, we'd gather for meals and family time, then head off to our separate spaces."

"Perfect combination of togetherness and privacy," she said, trudging behind me through the four foot drifts.

"It really was. Then Mel and Bent started staying in town, keeping the restaurant open during the winter and it was just my folks and me."

"And with the baby coming?"

"They're threatening to build a house on a lot they own beside her place. They'd been holding onto it, thinking they'd put in something touristy. Even money says they put in a storefront on the street level and live on the second floor. Maybe they'll build a bridge connecting it to Mel's."

"I'm sure your sister will appreciate that."

"My apartment is looking more and more attractive every day."

"You wouldn't come back out here by yourself if they move to town?"

"I'd be tempted, but when push comes to shove, I'm not that much of a hermit."

We reached the cabin and I stood aside to let her go in first. It was a large A-frame with one build-out on the side that housed the kitchen. On the other side, there was a glass-enclosed sunroom that held the hot-tub. A large living and dining space took up the center of the cabin with a ship's ladder leading to the loft bedroom.

"Heaven," said Olivia, inhaling deeply as she reached the loft and turned to look out the wall of windows. The two small cabins were tucked into the trees at the far side of the clearing and the rest of the view was the woods and the mountains behind them.

"Beautiful, isn't it?"

"It's spectacular. I'd never give this up to live in town, even a town as quaint as Coho Bay."

"It isn't town they're thinking about. It's the patter of grandbaby feet."

"That's a powerful incentive."

Chapter 7

The morning of Mrs. Nash's funeral dawned grey
and cold, but there was no snow in the forecast. Olivia
planned to spend one more night in Coho Bay, then
return to Minneapolis to finish her residency. I'd
offered to take her to the airport since there wouldn't be
another ferry for a week, but she'd already made
arrangements. "There's no reason for you to put
yourself out when Kenny's going anyway." I hadn't
been able to argue with logic like that.

I was standing in my new bedroom, which lacked
only paint on the walls to be complete. There was no
window because Dad knew I like it dark when I sleep.
Not that there was ever much light in the winter, but it
would also be warmer without a window and I did love
to sleep warm in the wintertime. "I'll help you cut out a
window in the spring," I told him when he joined me.

"You don't have to do that, Kit," he said, putting an
affectionate arm around me.

"You could sleep an extra half hour if you lived
here," Mom said from the doorway.

"Nobody's gonna get any sleep with a baby crying
all night," I countered.

"The baby will be sleeping through the night by
summer."

"C'mon, Dad." I headed downstairs, following my
nose to the dining room. I can be every bit as stubborn
as Mom and I was not going to sacrifice my
independence to gain a little extra sleep. Unless it

meant they would forego building a new house next door. I'd sacrifice to save my sister's sanity.

After breakfast, we walked over to pick up Olivia. She'd wanted to be alone on her last morning before saying good-bye to her grandmother forever. They waited on the boardwalk while I went around to the apartment. Olivia opened the door before I could knock and pulled me into the entryway for a hug. Her eyes were suspiciously red but she shook her head when I tried to say something. She threw her coat on over the somber black dress she wore and pulled the door shut behind us.

On the boardwalk, Frank had joined my family, having elected to sleep on his boat again last night. He offered one arm to me and the other to Olivia and we set off for the church. I loved its traditional Russian Orthodox white walls and green roof, with onion domed dormers topped by metal crosses. There was a steeple with a bell, added when the two protestant sects formed their own congregations, but the combination was charming. It was a bigger building than you would expect to find in a town our size so the Russians must have had high hopes when they founded Coho Bay to serve the fishing trade. None of the religious leaders lived in town and Mrs. Nash hadn't been a member of any of the churches, so Mayor Solokov had agreed to lead the service.

We sat with Olivia in the front pew, feeling oddly out of place since our family pew was further to the back. It was disconcerting to be so close to the altar and to the satin draped coffin in front of it. I squirmed in my seat, looking around as my friends slowly filled the seats in the sanctuary. Many people had known Mrs. Nash in passing, and she'd been coming up enough years to have earned honorary citizenship so the whole town had turned out. I smiled at Dan as he took a seat across the aisle and a few rows back. He smiled back at me, but his smile faded when Frank leaned over to me and whispered, "Nice turnout."

Olivia sat ram-rod straight, an island of misery in the sea of polite concern. Mel grasped her hand and leaned against her shoulder. Sophie Kakoweth, who manages the Nuntok tribe's craft shop during the season, took her seat at the organ and began to play the hymn my mother had requested, "Nearer My God, to Thee." We didn't know what music Mrs. Nash might have liked so we had chosen hymns we hoped would bring Olivia some comfort. As a tear welled in the corner of Olivia's eye, I knew we'd chosen well.

As the music faded, Solokov stepped to the right of the draped coffin. "Let us pray," he said. Heads bowed as he led us in the same simple prayer that had opened every funeral I'd ever attended. Afterward, he gave a surprisingly moving eulogy, so completely out of character that I knew my Mom had written it for him. It was such a lovely speech I couldn't fault her it.

We stood to sing "Rock of Ages." It was Mel's favorite and one the congregations had sung so many times the voices were strong and powerful around us, music filling the sanctuary. Olivia's voice, broken with emotion, blended with mine as we shared a hymnal. My dad talked about meeting Mrs. Nash and her husband the first year they'd come to stay with the Tilamus. He spoke about the close friendship between the two couples and how that friendship had continued after Doc had lost his wife and Mrs. Nash, her husband.

"That's a crock. This whole thing is one big, fat lie after another." Alex Tilamu was standing in the aisle, rocking on his feet as though he were standing on the deck of a ship. Murmurs rose across the congregation, sounding more excited than horrified.

"Alex, this is neither the time nor the place." My father's voice was calm, but the whispering intensified as it hit people who the speaker was.

Alex swore, causing a few of the older women to gasp. "You're all sitting here crying and singing for the woman who murdered my mother."

Dan stood up and took his arm. "Alex, that's enough."

Alex shook Dan off. "Who the hell are you?" There were more gasps and some nervous tittering.

Dan took Alex's arm again, trying to turn him around. "You can tell me all about it outside."

Alex shook him off again and steadied himself on a pew. "You can't shut me up. She killed my mother and then she went home and killed her husband so she could have my father."

At that, Olivia jumped up and whirled around, her eyes spitting fire. "Shut up, you lousy drunk! You didn't know my grandmother. You don't know what you're talking about."

That brought us all to our feet, funeral decorum forgotten. Voices raised again, but not in song, as townspeople started to take sides. Frank and Bent helped Dan drag Alex out of the church, while he hurled accusations in language that was making even the younger women gasp. It was nearly half an hour before the uproar began to die down and by then, the dignity of the service had been hopelessly broken. Solokov dismissed the congregation, which filed from the church, past the clinic and into the recreation hall where the ladies groups were serving lunch.

Only a handful of us stayed. The pall-bearers, part-time city workers dressed in their Sunday best, walked with the coffin out the back door to the cemetery. Mel and I put our arms around Olivia and half-carried her behind them. Those who'd best known Mrs. Nash followed us and by the time we gathered around the grave, the quiet of the cemetery and the sacredness of the ground into which they lowered the coffin restored peace.

Olivia stood beside the grave for a long while after everyone else had gone. I waited at a respectful distance, giving her space. She crouched down and picked up a handful of dirt, sprinkling it into the grave. Then she looked around her, then took the few steps to look down at the Tilamu graves. She put a hand on each stone and bent her head. She stood one more time by her grandmother's grave, then walked down the hill to meet me.

"What are those little houses?" she asked, pointing at doll-house-sized structures that adorned some of the graves. They were of differing shapes and sizes, painted in bright colors and obviously tended with loving hands.

"Spirit houses. When the Nuntoks bury a loved one, they cover the grave with a woolen blanket, then place a spirit house over the top. It gives their spirit a place to go before they make the journey to the other side."

"How lovely."

We started back toward the recreation hall. "The spirit houses are built to resemble something meaningful in the person's life."

"Do they take them down once the spirit has had time to make that journey?"

"No. I think by then, it's a comfort to those who've been left behind. One last show of respect for the person they lost."

"Is it only the Nuntoks who do it? Would it be rude or disrespectful for me to put up a spirit house for Gram?"

"I don't know whether the Nuntoks would mind, if it was out of love and respect, but I don't know that anyone's ever done it."

She was thoughtful as we walked but as we approached the hall, she hesitated. "Would it be terrible if I didn't go inside? I don't think I can face people."

"Nobody believes what Alex said. You could see he was drunk. He was just talking crazy."

"What if he's right?"

"Olivia! I know you hadn't known your grandmother long, but she was the sweetest person in the world. She'd never kill anybody."

"She killed herself," said Olivia, "and in the most violent way possible. I'm sure you never dreamed she could do that, and yet she did. We don't know what else she might have done."

I took her arm and waited until her eyes met mine. "Yes we do. Mrs. Tilamu died of cancer. Everybody in Coho Bay saw her suffering. As for Alex, he's got no call to be accusing anyone. All the time she was sick, he never came to visit her. Not once. He shook the dust off his feet when he moved away and he never came back. There's no mystery in her death and if Alex is wrong about her, he's wrong about your grandfather's death too."

"I want to believe that but I never knew my grandfather. I only know what my grandmother told me about his death and she certainly wouldn't have told me if she killed him."

It was too cold to stand outside arguing with her about something neither one of us had first-hand knowledge about. "I'll talk to Dan, but cancer is the only thing that killed Mrs. T."

She nodded and started across lots toward the apartment. Then she stopped and turned to look at me. "Tell your dad to hold off on fixing up the house."

My heart sank, but I tried not to let it show. "I'll let him know."

She trudged off through the snow, seemingly heedless of the cold. I was cold just watching her and I was wearing wool slacks with knee-high boots. In the recreation center people were seated at round tables or standing in line at the buffet, talking in subdued tones. By the curious looks people shot me, I had a pretty good idea what they were saying. My fingers fumbled as I tried to unbutton my coat. I looked for my family and saw my mother sitting at a table on the far end of the room, deep in conversation with Mayor Solokov.

I took a step toward her, but suddenly, I wanted to be anywhere but there. Ignoring my sister, who'd risen when she saw me come in, I turned and ran out. I gasped, desperate to fill lungs that felt like they'd gone flat. I wrapped my arms around a post and pressed my hot face against the cold metal.

I felt Mel's arms wrap around me. "Cara, are you all right? Are you sick?" I didn't answer so she tugged me away from the pole and sat down with me on the step in front of the recreation center. "You've been pushing yourself too hard. Gabby told me you could relapse."

I leaned against her, shaking, and dug for my voice. "I'm okay."

I heard the door open. My father squeezed himself onto the step next to us and put his hand on my knee. "Everything all right, honey?"

"I'm fine."

"She's sick, Daddy" said Mel, putting her hand on my forehead. "She's burning up."

"I'm not sick." I tried to bat her hand away.

Dad pulled me to my feet. "Let's get you home, Kit. Mel, would you ask Olivia to come over and take a look at her as soon as she's up to it?"

"Don't you dare bother her. It's just the stress of everything hitting me all at once."

"Are you sure?"

I managed to pull away from my father and stand on my own, only a little bit shaky. "I'm sure. It was just too hot in there. I'm fine now."

Mel looked unconvinced, but Dad came to my rescue. "You go back inside, Mel. If she asks, tell your mother we decided to go for a walk. Fresh air, that's what you need. Right, Kit?"

"Absolutely."

I'm not sure she believed us, but she didn't argue. Dad walked with me to the boardwalk. "Okay, spill," he said once we were out of earshot.

"Olivia's really upset, Dad. Could there be any truth in what Alex said?" I buried my hands in my coat pockets and kicked myself for forgetting my gloves.

"No. I don't think so."

I stared across at City Hall, wondering what was going on there. I took a step in that direction, but dad pulled me back. "Dan will tell us whatever we need to know. Right now, we'd only be in his way."

"How'd Alex get here? I thought Mom said he and his sister took the ferry out yesterday."

"Obviously he didn't."

"Why would Alex say a thing like that? He can't possibly think Olivia will give him the house now."

Dad shrugged. "You can't know what a drunk is thinking. What matters is Mrs. Nash didn't kill his mother."

"That's what I told Olivia but she's really shaken."

"Barging in there asking Alex a million questions you can bet Dan is already asking isn't going to help Olivia."

"I don't think Dan is asking any questions." I nodded to where he had emerged from City Hall and was walking toward us. When he was near enough I didn't have to shout, I asked, "Why aren't you asking Alex why he's trashing Mrs. Nash when she isn't even here to defend himself?"

"Hello to you too, Cara. Bob, could I bum a cup of coffee?"

"I'm happy to make you some," offered my father.

"Dad, I love you, but you make even worse coffee than Mom does."

"Yours isn't much better."

"I can make it," offered Dan.

"You'd be better off if you did," agreed Dad. We walked to the restaurant, Dad walking between us while I glowered at Dan and he pointedly ignored me. After hanging up our coats, he showed Dan where to find the coffee and the filters and we sat at the counter watching him.

"You look surprisingly at home back there, Dan," said Dad, watching him move around the space behind the counter.

"I did my time waiting tables." Coffee started, he leaned on the counter and looked sharply at me. "I heard you went home sick."

"Word spreads fast."

"When were you a waiter?" I asked.

"College. You look all right now."

"I thought you went to the police academy."

"One doesn't exclude the other."

Dad's head was bobbing back and forth between us. When neither of us spoke, ne nudged me. "Your turn, honey."

I glared at him, then looked at Dan. "Why are you here acting like Suzy Homemaker instead of in your office grilling Alex?"

"Because he's passed out in the holding cell."

"We have a holding cell? Kit, did you know we have a holding cell?"

"No, I didn't. I thought they just sent the drunks home to sleep it off."

"Alex doesn't have a home. At least not one they can send him to."

"You have a point."

Dan had been watching us in silence, waiting for us to run out of steam. "So you're not sick?"

There was a new sweetness in the tone of his voice. "I was just sick of people and I feel horrible for Olivia. Dad, she told me to have you hold off on fixing up the house."

"That's not good, but I'm sure she'll feel differently about it in the morning."

"Coffee?" Dan asked.

"With cream, thanks."

"Bob?"

"With pie if there's any left."

"Oooh, pie. Good idea, Dad. I'll go look."

"Sit down," said Dan. He returned with what was left of the last pie of the season and three plates. He set them in front of Dad and went to pour the coffee.

"You don't seriously think Alex is telling the truth, Dan."

He studied me as my father divvied up the pie. "You don't."

"Does that mean you do?"

"It means I try not to make up my mind until after I investigate. It's a cop thing."

Dad waved a fork at him. "Bias is the enemy of good science."

I rolled my eyes. "There's nothing to investigate. Mrs. Nash didn't kill anybody. End of story. Tell him, Dad."

"Did you know Clara Tilamu?" Dan shook his head. "She died when Cara was, oh first or second grade, wasn't it?"

"Something like that," I agreed. "She used to come with Doc when he made house calls. She smelled like vanilla."

Dad laughed. "The things kids remember. She was Doc's nurse. She'd hold down the kids so he could give them their shots."

"She did not!" I felt my face turning red as Dan smiled.

"She was a nurse?"

"I don't know if she had any formal training. She went with him on house calls and worked with him in his office."

"Tell me how she died. Cancer, I know, but what do you remember about her actual death?"

Dad put down his fork and closed his eyes. "I'm trying to remember when I first heard she was sick. About a year before she died, she spent time in the hospital and when she came home, everybody talked about her in whispers, but nothing was ever said straight out. You didn't talk about the Big C back then." He looked at Dan, who nodded encouragingly.

"She looked tired, but she didn't really seem sick. In the spring, she and Doc went south to visit their kids but they did that every few years. When they came home, it was shocking how ill she looked."

He stopped, closing his eyes again, but this time his expression was sad. "She died a few weeks later. I can't tell you exactly what happened, because I wasn't with her. Doc said she died in her sleep. The Nashes were staying with them and they were there when Clara died."

"I remember everybody crying," I added.

Dad patted my hand. "I suspect they did. She was well loved."

"What can you tell me about Alex?"

I looked at Dad, unconsciously chewing on my lower lip. "I don't know Alex very well," I said when he offered no response. "I'd never met him before yesterday, just talked to him on the phone."

"About renting out a house that he didn't actually own."

"Bizarre, isn't it? Actually, most of the time I didn't talk to Alex at all, but to his older sister, Anne. She seems to wear the pants in that family. She's the one who was with him yesterday, I suspect, though I didn't see her."

"It was Anne, all right. She's the middle sister," said Dad. "Aggie's the oldest, Agatha, but she never cared what happened to the house. It was always Alex and Anne."

"Agatha, Anne and Alex. What's up with that?"

I smiled. "I always wondered about that myself, but there's no telling what people will name their children."

"What about Mr. Nash?"

"I knew him only slightly," Dad answered. "That was long before Mel's place, of course. You only saw people in church back then, or town functions. He didn't mix much."

"What was he like?"

Dad hesitated. "It's only my impression and as I said, I didn't know him well. He struck me as one of those people who thinks he's...." Dad stopped, searching for the right words. "Some people were worth talking to and some weren't. Most of the people here in Coho Bay seemed to be among the ones who weren't."

"That would fit with what Olivia said about her grandfather disowning his own daughter because she married a black man," I said.

"He died the same year as Mrs. Tilamu?"

"Yes, though the deaths are completely unconnected, Dan."

"How did he die?"

"Mrs. Nash told us he was in a car accident."

"Cara told me she thought there was something romantic going on between Doc and Mrs. Nash."

"Not while they were both still married!" I said. "Nothing like what Alex insinuated."

"I know you believe that, but in my experience, kids notice things. They may not know what to make of them, but they pick up on things adults don't bother to see. What do you think, Bob?"

"You should ask Marcie. She's much more attuned to that sort of thing than I am."

I got up to bus the tables. "Looks like you can ask her now, Dan," I said, gesturing toward the door with the empty pie tin.

Mel excused herself to go upstairs and Bent went with her. Frank frowned when he saw Dan but my mother walked up to where he was standing and thrust her finger into his face. "Daniel, why are you sitting here eating pie when Alexander is making his ghastly accusations?" She looked around, as if expecting to see him sitting at one of the tables. "Where is the little snail?"

"Jail."

"Good."

Frank, sidled up to me and took the plates. "Let me help you with that, Boo."

I threw an annoyed glance at him but I hurried him into the kitchen and tossed them haphazardly into the dishwasher. Declining his offer to wash dishes, I rushed back out, not wanting to miss what my mother would say. By the time I got him back, Dan was putting on his coat. Frank, following me back into the dining room behind me, put his hands around my waist. I tried to pull away but he held fast. "Where are you going, Dan?"

"We're not speaking to him, Caribou."

I looked at my mother. Her face was frozen in anger. I must have missed something good. "Why aren't we speaking to Dan?"

The bell rang again as Olivia came in. She must have heard me because she looked at him with a puzzled expression. "We aren't speaking to you? Why not?"

"Ask her," he said, pointing at my mother. He zipped up his coat and waited, arms crossed, for her to answer.

"We are not speaking to Daniel because he chooses to believe a drunken, middle-aged hoodlum."

"You believe the guy at Gram's funeral?" asked Olivia, stepping away from Dan. "You actually believe what he said about her?"

"It's not my job to believe or disbelieve what anyone says," said Dan.

Mother cut him off. "Nor is it your job to dig up garbage about people on the say-so of a malcontent who never had the decency to visit his own mother when she was dying. He's just upset to find out that a lovely little house he's been neglecting for years isn't his to neglect after all."

"Marcie, don't you think it's strange that Doc would give his house to this woman?"

"That's my grandmother you're talking about."

"I'm sorry, Olivia. I'm not insinuating it was payment for killing his wife. I just think it was an odd thing to do. I can understand him thinking it was none of the town's business, but why wouldn't he tell his own children?"

"Because they were selfish ingrates who deserted him and his wife the minute they were old enough to do so," was Mom's answer.

"I thought you weren't talking to Dan, dear."

"I was speaking to Olivia."

I finally managed to slip free of Frank and put the counter between us. "Dan, why is it your job to investigate this? If Mrs. Nash killed herself, what does it matter why Doc gave her the house?"

"Because if she received the house as part of a conspiracy, that would invalidate the title."

"That is a civil matter, Daniel, not a criminal one. I told you, Dr. Tilamu gave Mrs. Nash the house because his children neither wanted it nor deserved it."

"Why not leave it to her in his will then?" asked Dan.

"I can answer that." Everyone turned to look at me. "If you put property in your will, it has to go through probate, as the house is doing now. His children could have challenged the will and tied it up in court for who knows how long. Give it to her while he's alive and he signs one piece of paper and it's done. Incontestably."

Olivia turned to my father. "Is that true?"

"That's why our children are on the title of every property we own. Saves a lot of grief."

"Enough of this. Spin your wheels tracking down non-existent crimes if you must, Daniel. I want to speak with Olivia about what it will take to bring her house into good repair."

"I can't do it, Marcie," said Olivia.

"Don't worry about Alexander's nonsense. Nobody who matters believes a thing he says. Now, Mr. Clarke has indicated to Caribou that he would support us making the house livable in order to sell so I'm sure he won't object to getting it ready for you."

"I appreciate all you've done, but I just can't move to Coho Bay with people thinking Gram may have been a murderer. That's what I came over to tell you. I'm sorry." She ducked out the door, leaving us in open-mouthed silence.

It didn't take my mother long to recover. "See what you've done, Daniel?"

"What I've done? How is this my fault?"

"You giving credence to that drunk's mean-spirited rant is depriving us of our one and only hope of securing a top-flight physician. I hope you're happy."

"Mom, I like Olivia too but you can't possibly know how good a doctor she is just because she's a nice person."

"Nonsense, Caribou. I spoke with her clinical supervisor and the dean of her medical school. They spoke glowingly of her. Even so, I'm so desperate I'd go after a bad doctor."

"Okay, but how is all this Dan's fault? Regardless of what he does, people will spend the winter talking about this and by spring, at least some of them will be convinced where there's smoke, there's fire."

"Which is why you are now going to devote yourself to proving Mrs. Nash's innocence, Daniel."

"I think I liked it better when you weren't talking to me, Marcie."

***

Dan left and my parents went upstairs to check on Mel. Frank followed me into the kitchen and leaned against the counter, watching me run water to wash the pots and pans from breakfast. "How do you prove someone is innocent of something that happened twenty years ago?"

"That's Dan's problem."

"It's ours too if it means Olivia doesn't want to move here."

"What do we care? We're young and healthy."

"In case you forgot," I said, easing a cooking pan into the hot, soapy water, "I almost died a few weeks ago."

"But you came through just fine."

"And young, healthy people get hurt around here. Hunting accidents, fishing accidents. That's how Mayor Solokov lost his hand."

"I didn't even know he lost a hand."

"He has a very good prosthesis. He was in commercial fishing and was helping process the day's catch when he got his hand caught in the slicer."

"Youch! When was that?"

"Before my time, but if Doc hadn't been on hand to stop the bleeding, Clem would have died. He'd never have made it all the way to Juneau." I tossed him a dish towel. "Make yourself useful."

He picked it up. "Clem doesn't really go with Solokov."

"His family is Russian."

"And the Clem part?"

"Short for Clemson."

"As in Go Tigers?"

"It was his father's alma mater and where his parents met. I think it's sweet."

"Maybe I'd better find out what kind of names you'd pick for our kids."

I gave him a sideways glance and noticed the sparkle in his eyes. "How about Cupcake?"

"Cupcake Baker? You're dooming her to a lifetime of therapy. What if we had a boy?"

"Just don't name him Bentley," said Bent, coming into the kitchen.

"How's Mel?" I asked.

"Sleeping. Why are we naming babies? You two got somethin' to tell me?"

"How'd you end up with a name like Bentley?" asked Frank.

"Bentley Milford Andrews, the third, to be precise. Old family name. Changed it to Bent when I went into the Navy."

"Sounds Southern."

"Virginian, born and bred, all the way back to colonial days."

"I didn't know that," I said, putting away the plates Frank had dried. "I mean, I knew your family was from Virginia but not for like, ever."

"That's because it isn't important," said Bent. "Where are you from, Frank? I know Seattle, but what about before that?"

"I've rambled around. I like Alaska though. It suits me."

"How are you liking working with Jack?" I asked. "Do you think you'll enjoy running the mill once he retires?"

Frank tossed the dish towel onto the counter and I picked it up, folding it neatly and hanging it on a rack without thinking about it. "I don't know whether I'll stick with the mill, but if I don't, I can always go back to taking tourists out to look at whales."

"But we need someone running the mill," I said, frowning. "Anybody can wrangle tourists."

"And anybody can run a mill," he said. "I'm just not sure it's for me."

"What did you do for a living before you moved here?" asked Bent.

"This and that. Little bit of anything that would pay enough to put a roof over my head. That's what I like about the boat. Water's different every day and most of the tourists are good people. Pays better than the mill too, and with a lot less work."

"What did Jack say when you told him?" I asked. "I know how much it hurt him when Johnny didn't want to work the mill anymore."

"There's nothing to tell. I'll take over the mill for now. I just haven't decided whether I'll keep at it or sell it and go back to my boat."

"Sell it?"

"It is a business, Cara," said Bent.

"But Jack isn't selling it to you, is he? I thought he was giving it to you."

"That doesn't mean I can't sell it to someone else. I'm not making a lifetime commitment to it."

He was right, but something about it made my skin crawl. It didn't seem fair to Jack for Frank to accept his generosity only to turn around and sell the business for a profit.

"The money doesn't matter to Jack. He's got all the money he'd ever need and more. He just wants to make sure somebody keeps the mill going and I'll make sure of that. Whether it's me or somebody else, why should it matter to him?"

"I suppose." Jack's heart had gone out of the business when his wife died. He'd staggered through, but he had long since lost his love for the feel of the wood in his hands.

"I gotta go." Frank pushed himself away from the counter and was gone without another word. It felt strange to be joking about babies one minute, only to get the cold shoulder the next.

"Hit a nerve with that one, little sister. You'd better watch yourself with him."

Chapter 8

Olivia left town at dawn, leaving the key to my apartment on the counter along with a note.

> *Cara, thank you so much. In spite of everything, because of the kindness shown me by you and your family, I will always have fond memories of Coho Bay. Please let your mother and Mayor Solokov know how much I appreciate their generous offer. While I would love to be able to accept, I just can't see a way to make it work with the cloud over Gram's head. I have no idea what to do about Gram's house, but when I figure it out, Mr. Clarke will let you know.*

I couldn't blame her, but I was sorry to lose her. Not only would it be hard to find a doctor with even half her skill, I would have liked to have her as a friend. She seemed like the kind of person who would have been fun to hang out with in happier times. I crossed the street to City Hall. Tammy grinned as she greeted me and told me Solokov was out when I asked to see him.

"Dan's here though," she said with a suggestive smirk.

"That's okay, I'll catch Clem later." I started to leave, but Dan came running out, hand on his gun.

"Stop using that panic button, Tammy, or I'll rip it out myself. What brings you here, Cara?"

I handed him Olivia's note. "I was going to talk to Clem, but Tammy says he isn't here today."

"Yeah, he went out with his son this morning. Sorry to see this," he said, giving the note back. "Marcie's gonna kill me."

"It's not your fault, Dan. Is there any chance you could clear Mrs. Nash?"

"I don't see how when there isn't any evidence a crime was ever committed. How do you prove somebody didn't do something that never happened? Gossips are always gonna find something to talk about, but I spent yesterday talking to everybody I could find who knew both couples. Mrs. Tiliamu died of cancer, just like it says on her death certificate. People remember that funeral like it was yesterday. They all agree both Doc and Mrs. Nash were torn up about it and that doesn't seem like the reaction of a couple of clandestine lovers and murderers. Not that it matters, everybody agrees Mr. Nash didn't seem broken up about it, but that could just be because nobody seemed to like him."

"They have the same impression of him Dad had?"

"Yep."

Tammy had been following our conversation. "Maybe Doc gave her something. To let her go peaceful like, ya know?"

"Legally, that would still be murder, but if anybody suspected it at the time, nobody's saying anything."

"That poor woman suffered something awful," Tammy said, nodding her head vigorously. "Nobody would've blamed the poor man."

"Is Alex sticking to his story now that he's had time to sober up?"

"He is, but he's not making any more sense than he did when he was drunk. He just keeps repeating his accusations and insisting Olivia has no right to his family's home."

"Not that he ever cared about that house." I snorted and Tammy giggled. "He and his sisters let that house fall apart. Why are they going all sentimental about it now?"

"Money does that to people," Dan said.

"When is he leaving? He isn't under arrest, is he?"

"Clem made him pay a fine and advised him to think twice before visiting Coho Bay again."

"Doc'll be turnin' over in his grave over it." Tammy made a clucking sound. For all her melodrama, she was right. I began to think my mother was right about why Doc would have disinherited his children.

"I need to borrow your boat, Cara."

I pulled myself out of my musings and stared at him. "Why?"

"Clem wants me to follow Alex to Juneau and make sure he gets on a plane, then suggest the boat rental company find an excuse not to rent to him again."

"He rented a boat? I thought he came on the ferry."

"His sister went back on the ferry day before yesterday. He says she washed her hands of him."

"Well, is it legal to ask somebody not to rent to him?"

"No. Can I borrow your boat?"

"The city really ought to buy a bigger boat for you. That little rig of theirs isn't much use once you get out of the mouth of the bay."

"Think how much money you'll be saving the taxpayers when you loan me your boat."

"I'll take you to Juneau."

"Cara, that's not necessary."

"Ooh, la," said Tammy. Dan glared at her and she went back to pretending not to listen.

"Let me call the university and see if those instructors I need to meet with will be available. If they say no, I'll give you the keys. Deal?"

"Fine. Call them. Alex is chomping at the bit and I'm running out of excuses to keep him here."

I hurried out, talking on my cell phone. Happily, the two professors were agreeable so when I got home, I took the steps up to my apartment two at a time. I hurried to throw clothes into a duffel bag. We weren't planning an overnight trip, but this time of year, it's best to be prepared. I stopped by Mel's to let her know where I was going, avoided the look Mom threw at me, kissed Dad, hugged Bent, grabbed the boat keys and was gone.

Fifteen minutes after I left City Hall, I met Dan on the dock. Alex was standing beside him, slouched over and looking like he'd had a rough night. He grumbled something when Dan told him to shove off, but he obediently climbed into his boat, one about half the size of The Sea Pallet so I knew I'd have to throttle down on this trip or he'd never keep up. Dan untied his line and tossed it onto the deck, then did the same for me as I fired up the engine, dutifully trailing the smaller boat.

"If you want to date Frank instead of me, I won't stop you." Dan hadn't said much during the first hour of our trip so his opening the second hour with this kind of threw me. "I won't be happy about it," he continued, "but I won't make it hard for you."

"Where'd that come from?"

"I never much liked the rule that says you can't say what you really think when you're seeing someone."

"In that case, I'm wishing we could talk about something else."

He laughed. "At least you're honest."

"I am seeing Frank. I guess. Just like I'm seeing you. If that's what you call it. I'm not ready to be exclusive, but I don't want that to sound like I'm a player because I'm not like that. Do you see why I don't like talking about this kinda stuff?"

Dan chuckled softly. "I didn't mean to put you on the spot. I'd like to keep seeing you and I don't expect you to stop seeing other men just because you're seeing me. I just wanted you to know I wasn't going to make it uncomfortable for you."

"So, you want me to see Frank?"

Dan came to stand behind me at the captain's chair. I kept my gaze locked on the boat in front of me as he put his hands on my shoulders. "It's too early for us to be exclusive. I get that." He started massaging and I had to rivet my eyes on the water to keep my focus. "I don't want to push you into thinking you have to choose between us."

"You always think it would be great to have men fighting over you. Not so much."

"He does seem the jealous type." He dropped his hands and took his seat again, never taking his eyes off me. "You shouldn't have to be somebody you're not or do something you're not ready for in order to be in a relationship."

"I don't know about that. Every guy I've ever been with always wanted me to be something."

"Like what?"

"Funnier, sillier. Certainly sexier." The moment the words were out, I wished I could pull them back.

"I think you're funny and silly. Also smart, honest and brave."

"Not sexy, huh?" What in the heck was I saying?

His answer was serious, thoughtful, not flirtatious or suggestive as Frank's would have been. "I've never gone for the kind of woman who dresses provocatively or paints her face and flounces around, showing off what God or a good plastic surgeon gave her. I mean, look at me. I'm no GQ model. Trust me, there are no six pack abs under here." He patted his belly. "Sexy starts with how you feel about someone not what they do to your blood pressure."

"Maybe you can say that because you've been married before. For me, sexy is… awkward."

"And it shouldn't be. Look, I've had sex with five women in my life. I'm not proud about it, but I have. Sex by itself is nothing. Body part A meets body part B. I've also made love to a woman I was deeply in love with and it's a very different thing. That's where you put your heart on the line, where you're sharing your soul with someone, not just your body."

"That was your wife?"

"Yes."

"But it didn't work out."

"No."

"Did she break your heart?"

"I wouldn't say that. You get to a point where you grow together, or you break apart."

"So maybe the whole soul to soul thing is over-rated."

"You think?"

"If you still end up alone, maybe I'm better off not being sexy."

"Cara, somebody's gonna touch your heart and you're gonna fall in love. It may be me or Frank or somebody you haven't even met yet, but when it happens, you won't have to wonder whether it's worth it. Everything's worth it for love."

"You're pretty romantic for a cop."

"Cops can't be romantic?"

"I read every book you dropped off for me. Nothing but hard-boiled, world-weary cops and private eyes. Nobody acts against their nature, Dan."

"You still talking about me?"

"I was but I was also thinking about Doc. He didn't kill his wife."

"Even though she was dying? It would have been a kindness."

"When people died around here, Doc would sit by their bedsides for hours, hold their hands, tell them stories, do what he could to make them comfortable but he never killed any of them."

"Physician assisted suicide may not be legal, Cara, but it's nothing new."

"I don't care! Doc wouldn't have done it. You said you talked to people who knew them. I was there. I never heard a whisper of it."

"You were too young for people to have whispered that kind of stuff to you."

"You'd be surprised what people will say in front of a kid because they think you won't understand."

"Like what?"

I thought about that for a while. Long-ago conversations drifted through my mind until one stuck. "Like Mrs. T telling Mrs. Nash that her own suffering would be over long before hers would be."

"What does that mean?"

I turned the boat over to Dan so I could focus on the memory until it was clear. "I was down by the water at low tide, exploring the tide pools. The two of them were sitting on a bench above me. You know the one Doc has next to the water?" Dan nodded. "Mrs. Nash was telling Mrs. T how sorry she was to see her suffering. It must have been the summer she died. Mrs. T told her there was more than one kind of suffering and at least hers would be over soon enough, while Mrs. Nash would go on suffering for the rest of her life."

"What did she mean by that?"

"I don't know. I didn't think much of it at the time, of course, and I hadn't thought about that conversation for years."

"You realize it makes it more likely that Doc killed his wife?"

"How so?"

"She knew her suffering would be over soon. Maybe they'd talked about him ending it for her when it got to be too much."

"She might also have known she was dying, Dan. That would be much more likely."

"It also makes it more likely Mrs. Nash went home and killed her husband, if that's why Mrs. T thought she'd suffer the rest of her life."

"He kills for love but with her it's just plain murder? I think you're wrong about both of them, Dan."

***

We made it to Juneau without delving more deeply into the nature of relationships, ours or anyone else's. I slid the boat into my usual slip at the marina and he jumped off, tying off the lines before helping me out of the boat. "We have to hurry," he explained as he set a blistering pace to reach the other end of the marina, where Alex would be turning in his rental.

There were times when I hated Dan. Here I was, panting like a racehorse about to be sent to a glue factory, while he—thirteen years older—was loping along not even breaking a sweat. We reached the sidewalk that connected the two areas and came to a stop since Alex was walking up the dock toward us. I leaned over, hands resting on my knees, gasping for breath as I tried to ignore the pain in my side.

"You okay?" asked Dan.

"Sure," I wheezed, my words coming out in short bursts. "Still…feeling…effects of…pneumonia."

Alex stared down at me. "What the hell's wrong with her? Scrawny dame like her oughta be able to run better'n that." He snorted at his attempt at humor.

"Leave it, Tilamu," warned Dan and Alex subsided.

There were many things I would like to have said, but every one of them would have required air, so said nothing. Dan and I had decided we'd share a taxi as far as the airport. I'd drop the two of them off at the terminal, then travel on to the University of Alaska campus. We'd meet back at the boat early in the afternoon so we could get home before dark.

My pulse had almost returned to normal by the time I reached the student center, where I'd arranged to meet the professors for coffee. I'd never been to UAS, having gone to the main campus in Anchorage, and I got lost a couple of times before I found the right building. In my defense, I was distracted by the sheer beauty of the campus. Seemingly carved out of the Tongass National Forest, it is situated along Auke Lake, with a backdrop of mountains and glaciers. I would have had a hard time studying if my dorm room had offered a view like that.

I didn't spare another thought for the view once the meeting started. I took notes as fast as my fingers could fly over the keyboard. I had initially envisioned one year-long fellowship, enabling an artist to live on Johnny's island, submersed in a master project or series of projects away from the distractions of day to day living. As we talked, the idea of having a summer arts intensive began to form. For one month during the summer, Coho Bay could host a number of artists who would live and work together, perhaps guided by experienced teachers or mentored by some of the artists whose work I'd been exhibiting. It was wildly exciting and insanely intimidating, all at the same time.

I hadn't watched the clock, noticing how late it had become only when my laptop battery died. I thanked the professors, promised to keep in touch, and ran across campus to catch a cab. Dan was waiting for me on the boat. "I'm sorry I'm late." The words spilled out as I scrambled to cast off and get underway.

Dan was quiet, but I was so excited to share every detail with him I didn't give him much chance to get a word in until we had traveled more than half the way home. When I finally took a breath, more because I was losing my voice than running out of things to say, I noticed he didn't seem to share my enthusiasm.

"No, it's not that," he explained, when I asked him about it. "The intensive thing sounds great. Hard work, with all you've already got going."

"I know. I don't know how I'm gonna pull it off."

"If it were me, I'd start small. One person this year. Get that up and running, then do the other thing—"

"The Intensive."

"Do that next year."

I frowned, deflated. "I suppose that would be more reasonable."

"That it does," Dan said, staring out at the water.

"I'm pretty dense about this sort of stuff," I said, "but there seems to be something bothering you."

Dan took a deep breath and huffed it out, but he didn't answer and my thoughts drifted back to the Intensive. How could I possibly devote a month during the height of the cruise ship season to something like that? Could we have it after the season? Would an October Intensive work? If artists were like the rest of us, working like crazy during the summer, trying to earn enough money to see them through the rest of the year, October might work better.

I almost missed it when Dan spoke. "I think Mrs. Nash might have been murdered."

"What? Why? Did the lab report come back?"

Dan shook his head. "I stopped by the boat rental when I got back to the marina."

"To illegally strong-arm them into not renting to Alex again."

"To let them know it might be better for everybody if they found a good excuse not to have a boat available if he comes back."

"Uh huh. Did they go for it?"

"On the record? No."

"And off the record?"

"Turns out this wasn't the first time he'd rented a boat from them."

"When did—Oh, Dan. You don't mean that Alex..." I stopped. Alex might be an alcoholic and a creep, but was he a murderer?

"Rented a boat the last week of the season. That's exactly what I mean."

"That's crazy. Alex hasn't set foot in Coho Bay since he left town thirty years ago and he didn't even know Mrs. Nash. Why would he come all the way up here and shoot her with her own gun?"

"Whoa, deputy. Slow down. I never said he shot her."

"Tell me that's not what went through your mind when you found out he'd been here."

"I don't know for certain he took the boat to Coho Bay."

"Yeah, right. I'm sure after all these years he just had a hankering for some Alaskan salmon and decided to go fishing. C'mon, Dan!"

Dan laughed. "I can't afford to make assumptions. I have to follow where the facts take me."

"That's what I'm doing."

"No, you're putting one and one together and getting six."

"So what do you get?"

"If Tilamu did come to Coho Bay, maybe somebody saw him."

"So you can prove he was there."

"That's right. Had anything changed about the property? Taxes going up? Mrs. Nash threatening not to rent next year?"

"The furnace broke down, but he didn't come up when the roof leaked or the water heater went out or when I called about any of the hundred other things that were falling apart. I can't imagine the furnace would bring him running."

"That's another good point."

"Are you going to ask Alex?"

"Never ask a suspect a question unless you already know the answer."

"They teach you that in the Police Academy?"

He shook his head. *"To Kill a Mockingbird.* If it was good enough for Gregory Peck, it's good enough for me."

"That was the movie. Didn't you read the book?"

"There was a book?"

I looked sideways at him. "Okay, Einstein. Who would know why he came up?"

"You're full of good questions today."

I made the turn into the mouth of Coho Bay as the sun began to sink on the horizon. "What we need are some answers."

Chapter 9

There was nothing resembling a romance novel cover about the look on Frank's face as Dan and I pulled up to the dock. As Dan tossed him the line, I decided Frank's face would have been more at home on the cover of a thriller.

"Evening, Frank," said Dan as he climbed out and reached back to offer me his hand.

Frank, who'd tied off the line faster than any two men I knew, held out his hand to me as well. I stood for a moment, looking up at the two men, who once again reminded me of snorting and pawing bull elk competing for the attentions of a cow. I shook the image from my mind, less because the men didn't resemble elk than because I didn't like to think of myself as a cow.

I reached out for both hands and allowed myself to be hoisted out of the boat and dropped onto the dock with considerably less grace than I would have liked. "Hello, Frank," I said with what cheerfulness I could muster. "What brings you out here?"

Frank looked over my head at Dan, who cleared his throat and touched my arm. "I have some phone calls to make, Cara. If you'll excuse me."

I watched him retreat up the dock until Frank stepped into my line of sight. "I was moving my things into your apartment," he said. "I saw the boat come in and thought I'd see if you needed any help."

"Help with...?"

"Most folks load up on supplies whenever they go into Juneau." He looked into the empty boat. "Got anything stowed in the cabin?"

"No, but thanks for asking. I really should have done some shopping. I didn't even think about it. I was too excited."

A line at the corner of Frank's mouth twitched. "About what? I thought you were just a taxi service for that creep."

"He's not a creep, Frank." I started up the dock.

"You're defending him? After what he said at that old lady's funeral?"

"You're talking about Alex? I'm not defending him, but sometimes grief and anger can warp a person."

Frank snorted. "Pickled in his case."

"Anyway, that isn't what I was excited about. I had a great meeting with the art professors at the university. They gave me all kinds of advice and pointed out things I hadn't even thought about." I climbed the wooden steps from the dock to the boardwalk and leaned on the railing, looking across the road to where my gallery stood. "Johnny would have loved doing something like this. There were times when I could almost feel him there today, getting worked up about all the emerging artists we're going to be able to help."

Frank sat down on the back of a bench that looked out on the bay, his feet on the seat, resting his arms on his knees, watching me with a smile playing across his face. "You look happier than I've seen you in a long while."

"Jack would be happy too. I should drive out there and tell him."

"I wouldn't."

I crossed to the bench and climbed up to sit beside him. "It's okay, you know. I've known Jack all my life.

He's never been the life of the party, but he's always been a decent guy at heart."

"He hides it well." We sat in silence, staring out at the bay. "I told Jack I couldn't do it."

"I thought you were gonna sell the mill if you decided you didn't like it."

"I got to thinking about what you said. Anyway, he can sell it himself if he wants to."

"I hope he finds somebody. I don't know what we'd do around here without that mill."

"Might slow down that new house your folks have been talking about."

I laughed. "Don't tell Mel that, she'll get Bent to torch the place."

"You mad?"

"About what?"

"Me not sticking it out at the mill."

"Not if you're not happy there." I waited but he didn't seem to have anything more to say. It was cold on the bench with the wind blowing off the water so I hopped down. "I'd better get going."

"I'll walk you home."

I threw a glance over my shoulder, wondering about the phone calls Dan was making, but I took the arm Frank offered. "The first thing I need to figure out is whether I should offer a full year on the island as I'd originally thought or whether I should break it into shorter time periods in order to help more artists."

***

"Don't you agree, Caribou?"

I jumped and blinked, trying to recall my mother's question, but there was nothing there. "I'm sorry, Mom."

She took off her reading glasses and examined me. I squirmed, feeling a sudden kinship with the specimens under her microscope. "Tell me."

"I'm just not sure whether I can pull off the Intensive this year, that's all."

"No, that is very far from all, young lady, because that was the topic of our conversation and you were nowhere in the vicinity."

"It's really not fair for mothers to read minds."

"Hey," said Mel, her eyes brightening, "does that mean I'm going to be able to do that with little Irving here?"

"Irving?" I asked, thankful for the diversion.

"It changes," answered my mother, "depending on her mood. Now, Caribou, we are not going to accomplish anything with your mind a million miles away. Tell me what's troubling you."

"It's men," supplied Mel.

"It is not!"

"I should think not. Where the men in your life are concerned, there really is nothing to discuss."

"I agree."

"You're going to marry Daniel and that's all there is to it."

"I thought you hated Dan."

"I don't hate him, Melody. I just don't trust him."

"But you want Cara to marry him."

"Sitting right here, guys."

"I've had an opportunity to become better acquainted with Franklin and I've decided he's not the right man for Caribou."

"Cut it out. I'm not marrying anybody."

"Ever?" asked Mel.

"Are you a lesbian, Caribou?"

"Mother!"

"It would explain why you've persisted in remaining single." I put my head in my hands, something I seemed to be doing a lot lately, but she kept on talking. "That nice young doctor is a lesbian. Perhaps you should marry her."

I looked up. "Olivia? Olivia's not gay."

"My dear, you simply must start paying more attention to the people around you."

"You are making my head hurt."

"Are you not feeling well?"

"I'm fine. Can we get back to the Intensive?"

"Mom, I think you're wrong about Olivia," said Mel.

"No dear, I'm sure of it."

"Did she tell you she was gay?"

"Mel, don't encourage her."

"Of course not," said Mom.

"Then I think you're reading her wrong."

"Time will tell. Caribou, are you ready to tell us where your mind has been?"

I gently banged my forehead against the table. "If you must know, I was thinking about Alex."

"Why?"

"Mel, did you see Alex in town at the end of the season?"

She dropped her pen. "Are you saying he shot Mrs. Nash?"

"I'm not saying anything. I'm just asking if you saw him. Or maybe heard somebody else talking about him being here." I wasn't sure I was supposed to say anything, but if Dan were going to ask around town about him, it was a safe bet he wouldn't get too mad about it.

"It's unseemly of you to ask questions like that, Caribou. You can ruin a man's reputation."

"He ruined it himself at the funeral, Mother."

Mom ignored Mel and looked at me with her *I know what you're thinking* eyes. "Unless you have a good reason to believe he was here."

I was on thin ice here, but I had to think Dan would be getting a similar response from the people he was calling on so I decided it wouldn't hurt to tell them. "Alex rented a boat, just like the one he had yesterday, at the end of the season." Mom sat back in her chair and Mel whistled under her breath. "I know. Crazy, isn't it? Why would Alex suddenly come here after all these years and why would he kill a woman he didn't even know?"

"Well, he must have at least known of her, Caribou, or he wouldn't believe she killed his mother and her own husband to marry his father."

"But she didn't marry Doc, Mother. They had years to fall in love if they were going to, but every summer, she lived in the house alone and he lived in the cabins."

"Which begs the question, why would he say things that are obviously untrue at the poor woman's funeral? It only served to bring attention to the fact that he was in Coho Bay when she was killed."

"You think he just made that stuff up?" I asked.

"How could he know about her husband if he didn't know her?"

"He may have been at the funeral for some time before he spoke. Everything he said about her, he could have learned from the eulogies."

"I hadn't thought of that." I mulled over what Mom had said. "Then we're back to why he would come to the funeral at all."

"That is the key," said Mom. "Find the answer to that question and you will know whether and why he would kill Mrs. Nash."

***

Both Dan and Frank showed up for dinner that evening, but Mom directed them to opposite ends of the table and placed me in the middle with Mel on one side of me and Dad on the other. "I understand that both of you are interested in my daughter," she told them as I stood there wishing for the floor to open up and swallow me, "but that is no reason to forget your manners. If you cannot control your innate competitive natures, we shall have to set up an alternating meal schedule."

I could die. I could just die, but the strange thing is, it worked. Maybe Dan had a point about not beating around the bush when it came to matters of the heart, but for whatever reason, it worked. The conversation was lively and when Mom and I cleared the dishes and brought out coffee and blackberry cobbler, I'd begun to relax and enjoy myself.

"Mel, you've outdone yourself on this cobbler," said my dad as he reached for a second serving.

"You and Mother picked the fruit," she told him, "I just grabbed it out of the fridge."

"It's a shame there won't be any more this year," said my mother. "It got too cold, too fast for my liking. I'm going to have trouble digging my carrots and potatoes out if it doesn't melt soon."

"A little freeze gives them flavor, Marcie," said Dan, leaning back after finishing his cobbler.

"Do you garden, Daniel?"

"I do."

"You do?" I asked.

"Don't look so shocked. I like good food as much as the next guy and it's way cheaper to grow my own than ship it in."

"That's true," said Mel. "If I had the time, I'd start a greenhouse and grow fresh produce for Bent."

"Hey, that's what you and Mom could do with the empty lot next door," I said, winking at him. "Start a greenhouse."

"That's not a bad idea, Kit."

"We shall see, Robert." My mother's tone signaled the end of that topic. "Daniel, were you able to find anyone who could verify that Alexander Tilamu was in town at the end of the season? Did anyone give you an idea what he was doing here?"

Dan looked at me and I raised my hands. "It wasn't a secret, was it?"

"It isn't now. Do any of you know a man named Dixon?"

We shook our heads and Dad asked, "Should we?"

"I haven't found anybody who saw Alex in town, but I did find a couple of people who said this Dixon guy came around late in the season asking them if they'd be interested in selling. Offered them decent money, too."

"Could it have been Dickerson?" I asked.

"Maybe. Nobody I talked to kept his card."

"I had a developer call about the Tilamu house. I wondered how he knew it might be coming on the market. I told him he needed to speak with Mr. Clarke. His name was Dickerson, but he didn't tell me he'd seen the property."

"You get a lot of random calls from developers who want to buy stuff sight-unseen?"

"Actually, she does," said Dad. "Since the cruise ships started coming, it's made property more desirable. People see houses on satellite mapping and call City Hall to find out who the owners are. Tammy sends them to Cara."

"Not that anybody ever wants to sell," I added, "but if the Tilamu house does go on the market, it'll go fast."

"So this Dickerson guy was asking about the Tilamu house?"

"Not by name, but he had an accurate enough description of it."

"Do you still have his number?"

"I should." I pulled out my cell phone and started thumbing through incoming calls. Before Dan could stop me, I hit *call back*.

A man answered on the third ring. "Ms. King? Do you have any news for me about that house?"

"Have you spoken with the executor?" Dan shot me an angry glare, but Frank and my family leaned forward to catch my end of the conversation.

"I called that attorney. He told me if the house went on the market you'd let me know."

"Well, it may. The new owner is debating whether to fix it up or sell it outright."

"If it helps, tell her not to go to any expense. I'll buy the house as-is."

"I'm not sure that's wise. The house has not been well maintained."

"It's a dump," he said bluntly, "but I'm not interested in the house. It's the land and the location I'm after."

"I'm sorry. I hadn't known you'd had an opportunity to tour the property."

"I was up there a few weeks ago and met the woman who was living in it."

"Mrs. Nash?"

"I didn't catch her name. Older lady."

"Could you hold on for just a second?" I hit the mute button and passed the phone to Dan. "He was here a few weeks ago and spoke with Mrs. Nash. I thought you'd better take it from here."

"Ya think?" His expression was still angry, but he took the phone and unmuted. "Mr. Dickerson, this is Dan Simmons. Ms. King thought it might be best for you to speak to me."

Dan got up from the table as he spoke and walked into the kitchen. I could hear him talking, but I couldn't make out what he was saying. We sat staring at each other. I doubted anyone else could hear the conversation any better than I could, but nobody seemed to want to say anything on the off chance that someone could. When the kitchen doors swung open, we all spoke at once.

Dan held up his hands, "Stop, stop, stop." He gave me back my phone and took his seat.

"Well?" I asked when I couldn't stand it anymore.

"The apparent owner brought him out to look at the Tilamu house. When they got to the house, there seemed to be a disagreement between the owner and the woman who was living in the house about who owned the property. He absented himself from the argument and walked around, knocking on doors and talking to other property owners. He stopped by the house on his way back to the marina but there was no one there. He waited for the owner to show up, but when he didn't, he hopped the ferry back to Juneau."

"The apparent owner?" I asked.

"Alexander Tilamu."

I slapped the table. "We've got him!"

"We've got something. We haven't got enough."

"What more do you need?" asked Frank and everyone turned to look at him. "What? I like a mystery as much as the next guy."

"Well, the mystery is solved," Mom declared. "Yes, yes, Daniel. I know you still have to find enough evidence to convince a jury, but we shall leave that to you. Melody, you are falling asleep at the table."

"I am pretty tired," Mel admitted with a yawn. She and Bent got up to clear the tables.

"I'll do that for you, Mel."

"Nonsense, Caribou. You have guests. Robert and I are perfectly capable of washing a few dishes."

My dad looked first at Frank, then at Dan and finally at me before he shrugged and started gathering up the dishes. He and Mom took them into the kitchen and left me sitting in the middle, between the two men. "Well this is awkward," I said as soon as they'd gone.

"I have to go," said Dan, getting up.

I stood too, but Frank kept his seat. "Don't go on my account, Daniel."

Dan gave Frank a look but I couldn't read his thoughts. He turned back to me. "I need to write this up and see if I can persuade a judge to issue an arrest warrant."

"I thought you said you didn't have enough."

"To get a conviction, no, but I might have enough to get him up here." I walked him to the door and stood while he buttoned up his coat. He ran a finger along my cheek. "I'll stop by tomorrow."

I waited to see if he'd kiss me, but he didn't. I suppose with Frank for an audience that would have been bad. Dan looked over my head and nodded at his rival. "Night, Frank," he said, and then he was gone. I locked the door behind him and watched him walk up the boardwalk toward City Hall.

"Well, that's that," said Frank, his voice sounding loud in the empty room. "Crazy, just crazy."

I walked slowly back to the table. "So I guess all the talk about Mrs. Nash killing his mother was just a smoke screen. Alex killed that poor, sweet old woman over a house."

"Greed, Cara. Oldest motive in the book." Frank took my hand when I reached him and I sat down beside him.

"Maybe now Olivia will want to move here."

"There you go, there's a bright side to everything." He stroked my hand with the tips of his finger and though the touch was innocent, the look in his eyes was decidedly not. His touch awakened something Dan's had not. "I want to see you tomorrow."

"I'd like that."

"Can't take you to dinner, because there isn't anywhere to go." He gestured toward the empty dining room.

"Let's go snowshoeing. It's perfect weather for it."

"I don't have shoes."

"You can borrow Bent's."

"It's a date."

Chapter 10

Dan stopped in after breakfast to let me know the prosecutor didn't think there was enough evidence to go before the judge. "He told me to wait for the lab report."

"What good will that do?" I asked. I was doing dishes and, not that I'm not always happy to see Dan, but he also gave me a good excuse to toss Mel the dishtowel and go sit in the dining room.

"I sent his prints to the lab. We'll see if they can place him at the house."

"When did you get his... oh, when you arrested him. But you already know he was there."

"I have one man's word for it. Nobody else in town seems to have seen Alex. Heck, for all I know Dickerson shot her when she wouldn't sell to him."

"Oh honestly. You don't get far as a developer if you shoot everybody who won't sell."

"I also only have his word for it that he's a developer."

"You said people hadn't kept his cards. You didn't say he didn't have them. Nobody prints cards on the off chance they'll need them to establish an alibi."

"They do in Agatha Christie novels."

I stared at him. A slow grin started to spread across his face. "Dan Simmons. Have you been reading Agatha Christie?"

He pulled out a battered copy of *Murder on the Orient Express.* "I inherited my uncle's book collection. Thought I'd take it for a spin."

"I bet you liked that one. Did you guess the killer?"

"Did you?"

"Not the first time."

"It's cheating to guess the killer on the second time through."

"That's not what I meant. It's just that she's so subtle when she drops hints, sometimes I go back and read it again once I know who the killer is just to see if I can pick up on it. It's a lot easier when you already know who the killer is."

"I would think."

"Don't make that face at me. It'll be easy for you too, now that you know who killed Mrs. Nash, to go back and find proof."

"You think so?" He crossed his arms and leaned on the table. "What do you think I should be looking for? Let me see what you've got, mystery girl."

"Fingerprints on the gun. He couldn't wipe them off if he was staging a suicide because that'd be a dead giveaway that she couldn't have shot herself."

"Dead women wipe no prints. Got it. What next?"

I stared out the window, thinking. "If he shot her, you'd think he'd have blood on his clothes. It's a wonder nobody noticed."

"It was cold the last day of the season. He'd have probably worn a coat."

"But he had to have changed at some point. You can't wear a coat through the security line at the airport and you'd think they'd have stopped him if he had blood on his clothes."

"Good point, Sherlock. I'll have to give that some thought. If he brought along a change of clothes, it would be premeditation." His face fell. "But if you bring clothes, why would you take a chance on the victim providing the murder weapon?"

"How'd he get a gun on the plane? I really think it had to be a crime of opportunity. You see the gun, you act. He might have had an overnight bag for the flight and it came in handy."

"In which case, the clothes are in the water between here and Juneau."

"I would think so. What about motive?"

"Money."

"Yes, but that makes it all the more likely it was a spontaneous thing. Alex brought this developer up to sell him the property, then he finds out it isn't his to sell."

"Unless he kills her."

"That obviously didn't make it his again. Maybe he got away with renting a house he didn't own, but even he would know it would come up in a sale. If he killed her over it, it was because he was angry and in shock."

"I see what you mean. I need to find out if the Tilamu heirs knew the house wasn't theirs and why they suddenly wanted to sell after all these years."

"You might try talking to Aggie."

"Aggie?"

"Agatha Kirby. She's the oldest of the three."

"Remind me. She's the sister who came up with Alex?"

"No, that was Anne. Anne Buchanan. All my dealings have been with Anne and Alex. I called Aggie once, out of desperation when I couldn't get them to authorize some repairs. She told me she washed her hands of that house and didn't want to have anything to do with it."

"Sounds like she knew about the ownership."

"Or just that there's a rift in the family. When I asked Dad about it, he told me Aggie was pretty close to her parents but once her mother died, as far as he knew, Doc never heard from her again. Said it broke his heart because it was Aggie he and his wife went to visit before she died."

"Do you have her number? Or are you planning to conveniently call her before you give it to me like you did the developer?"

I blushed. "Sorry. I got caught up in the moment." I went into the kitchen and pulled my keys from a hook by the back door. Returning, I put them on the table in front of him. I grabbed an order pad from behind the counter and neatly wrote a series of numbers. "I'm going to make it up to you by letting you go to my office and get the numbers out of my files. Here's the alarm code. Just re-arm and lock up when you leave. You can drop the keys back anytime."

He picked up the code but didn't look at it. "That's assuming you won't call her first from here."

"Dan, I've called Aggie one time in my whole life and that was from my office. I don't have her number on my cell phone." I pretended to be hurt, because that was exactly what I might have done, had I had her number on my phone.

He laughed. "Come on. We'll call her from your office. She might pick up the phone quicker when she sees it's you than if she sees the police are calling."

"Well, if you really need me…" I didn't bother to finish. I ran back to the kitchen, where Mel was just finishing putting the dishes away, and tossed my apron in the hamper. "Gotta go help Dan."

"I thought you had a date with Frank today."

"Not until later."

She shook her head. "For starting out life as a wallflower, you're certainly making up for lost time."

"This is business, Melly." I hugged her, careful not to bump the bump. "We're trying to nail down Alex's motive."

"And Dan needs your help to do this?" she said, but I was already out of the kitchen.

***

"That was no help," I said, slumping back in my chair after hanging up the phone. Aggie's daughter had answered the phone, telling us her mother was on a cruise and wasn't due back for three more days. "Who cruises in October?"

"I don't want this to come as a surprise to you, Cara, but there are other places people cruise to besides Alaska."

I glared at him. "Nobody I know."

"The Caribbean, Hawaii." I threw a pencil at him. "Asia, Australia…"

"What are you, a travel agent?"

"Haven't you ever wanted to go on a cruise? Watching all these people all these years getting back on their ship and sailing away. Haven't you ever wished you could sail with them?"

"Truthfully? No. You know what they say about cruisers. The newly wed and the nearly dead."

"Oh come on, you've met enough people from cruise ships to know that's not true."

"So where would you go if you could sail away?"

"Tahiti."

"Just like that. No thought, just *Tahiti*."

"What's wrong with Tahiti? Tropical breezes, warm ocean, island music."

"Island music?"

"You know what I mean. Ukuleles, drums. Stop looking at me like that. I think it sounds nice."

"Okay."

"You might like taking a cruise. People waiting on you, buying souvenirs instead of selling them."

"Dan, I don't sell souvenirs. Is that what you think of the work I carry?"

"It was just an expression."

"Buying souvenirs is not an expression."

"You know what I meant. You wait on people all day, every day but Thursday, hoping they'll buy your fine works of art. Wouldn't it be nice to turn that around and have somebody wait on you?"

I gave it some consideration. Cruisers always seemed happy coming off the ship, except a few bad apples but you would get that anywhere. Some people seem determined to go through life with a frown on their face. "I suppose I could try it. Someday. So what do we do now?"

"I'm going to call the boat rental and see if they found anything unusual in the boat Alex rented last month."

"Like a bag of bloody clothes?"

"Like anything they made a note of in the files, or anything for the lost and found. Then I'm going to start looking into this developer."

"Dickerson."

"Confirm his travel dates, make sure he's on the up and up."

"What about Anne?"

"If she's close to Alex, I don't want to tip my hand by calling her. I'm taking a big enough chance calling Agatha."

"I know, but she was with him the day before the funeral. My Dad thinks she must have taken the ferry out, and I guess that's true since Alex was alone the next day, but I do wonder what she was doing here. She lives in Montana so obviously the trip was planned. Why?"

"Good question. I'll take a look at her too."

***

I stood watching as Frank stumbled into Bent's snowshoes. "Need help?"

"I've got it," he said, trying to get his boot to catch, as you would if you were stepping into skis.

"It doesn't work like that," I said, holding out my foot so he could see how my snowshoes were attached. "You strap them on."

He bent back over his boot and was able to wrap the strap around the heel this time. He held up one foot, shook it and seemed satisfied enough when the snowshoe didn't fall off to strap on the other. He made quick work of that, now that he'd seen how it was done, and before long, we were trudging up the near side of the bay on a path that would take us past the cannery.

"You're pretty good at this, especially for a first time, Frank."

"I used to do some cross country skiing," he shrugged. "It's not too different."

"It's way different. But you're doing well anyway."

"What were you and Dan doing at the gallery this morning?"

I glanced at him, but he was looking straight ahead. "You shouldn't be worrying about what I might be doing with him anymore than he should ask what I'm doing when we're together."

"He asked you what we did last night?"

"No."

We went along without talking and I surrendered myself to the beauty of the day. Snowshoeing when I had to in order to get from point A to point B is an entirely different thing than doing it for pleasure. I breathed in the crisp air and was thankful for my sunglasses, which blunted the glare from the sun bouncing off the untouched snow. The cannery was closed this time of year and I noticed the fishing boats were either gone, looking for crab in the northwest, or hoisted from the water to dangle on boat lifts through the winter.

"How's your murder investigation going?" he asked as the path entered the woods past the cannery.

"Up and down. Dan's trying to tie down details while he waits for the state lab report. He's hoping that will give him proof Alex was in the house. Maybe we'll get lucky enough he left his fingerprints on the gun."

"He shot the old lady with her own gun?"

"That's what it looks like. If Dan has the ballistics report, he hasn't shared it."

"So your theory is he got so mad at her, he picked up her gun and shot her? Why'd she have the gun out anyway?"

"Maybe he threatened her."

"Your developer, what's his name?"

"Mr. Dickerson and he's not my developer."

"This Dickerson guy told you Alex brought him all the way out here with the idea of selling him the place so obviously, Alex assumed his family owned the house."

"Dan's trying to confirm that, but Aggie's off on a cruise, of all things."

"Dickerson said there was an argument between Alex and Mrs. Nash about which one of them owned the house, so he skipped out and went to find someone else who'd sell their house to him."

"That's what he told Dan, but he's checking up on Dickerson too, in case he's the one who killed Mrs. Nash."

"Huh. He hears her tell Alex the house is hers and she'll never sell so he slips back after Alex leaves, somehow gets her gun and shoots her, hoping to snap up the house from her heirs?"

"Does sound silly when you put it like that."

"He did call you awfully quick after you'd found the body, though. How'd he know she was dead?"

I stopped walking. "I can't remember if he knew or not. He said he was interested in the house, described it, and asked if the owners might be willing to part with it. I told him he'd have to talk to Mr. Clarke."

"Still seems fishy to me."

"It does, kinda. Anyway, Dan must think so too because like I said, he's checking up on Dickerson."

"So, what's your guess why Doc gave the house to that woman? You think it was payment for killing his wife like Alex said?"

"No." I started shoeing again and Frank fell in beside me. "Doc would never do that."

"Then he was having an affair with her."

"He wouldn't do that either, and as Mel pointed out, they never got married and they had ample opportunity. That couldn't have been it."

"When did he sign over the house to her?"

"A few years after his wife died."

"So what happened in his life around that time? What changed between Doc and his kids?"

"I was just a kid then, Frank. I don't know. I've never heard of anything." My phone started ringing so I sank down onto a fallen tree and answered it.

"Cara King? It's Agatha Kirby."

"Mrs. Kirby? My goodness, I thought you were on a cruise."

"We had a lovely ten days. We're in Miami for the next couple of days, then we're heading home. My daughter called me because she said your call sounded important."

"I appreciate you calling me back. I don't know if you ever met Mrs. Nash, the woman who's been renting the Tilamu house for so many years?" There was silence on the line. "Mrs. Kirby?"

"Yes, I heard you. I never met the woman."

There was something in the way she said, 'the woman' that made me wonder. "Well, she died recently and … I'm not sure how to say this, but I checked the land records and it seems she owned the house."

There was another silence. "Is that what you called to tell me?"

"Well, no. I called because, well, Alex was here."

"My brother? In Coho Bay? When was this?"

"He was here a few days ago," I said, deciding not to mention that we knew he'd been here when Mrs. Nash was killed.

"How very strange. I haven't spoken with Alex in years. What was he doing in Alaska?"

"He came to take a look at the house."

"Why on earth would he do that?"

"It seems, ma'am, he was under the impression that he—well, that the three of you—owned the house."

I waited. I had counted to five by the time she answered. "I imagine he did think so."

"But you knew otherwise?"

"When no one contacted me about probate when my father died, I assumed he'd left the house to Anne and Alex. I told you when you called me about it, didn't I, that I washed my hands of the place."

"I assumed you just weren't interested in it. It isn't as though there was very much money from the rent, especially split three ways."

"No, Miss King, I simply didn't care. This will probably come as a shock to you since everyone thought my father was a saint, but I hadn't spoken to him in years when he died. After my mother's death, I just couldn't bear to look at him."

"Your mother had cancer."

"Yes, she did. And she would have survived that cancer if he'd let her stay with me in D.C. instead of dragging her back to that god-forsaken hell-hole. I'm sorry. I'm sure you wouldn't understand."

"I understand that many people leave town when they need medical treatment."

"Exactly. But my father thought he could treat Mom as well as any cancer hospital and she didn't want to hurt his feelings. Hurt his feelings, Miss King! My father as good as murdered my mother when he took her back there."

"That must be why Alex told us his mother was murdered."

I hadn't realized I'd said that aloud until she answered. "Alex never took his head out of a bottle long enough to care how our mother died, and Anne wasn't much better. Oh, she doesn't drink, but she makes excuses enough to keep Alex from ever having to stand up and be a man."

"I thought Anne lived in Montana."

"She did, until her husband died. He left her well enough off, that is, until Alex got hold of her. She moved to Washington to take care of him and I told her she was making the biggest mistake of her life. That's when she stopped talking to me. Frankly, Miss King, it pains me to say this but my life has been more peaceful without either of them in it."

"I'm so sorry."

"Do you have brothers and sisters?"

"I have one sister."

"Well, I hope you have better luck with yours."

"So, as far as you knew, your siblings owned the Tilamu house?"

"Until you told me otherwise. Who does own it?"

"Mrs. Nash."

"Really." There was a sharp intake of breath. "She and her husband bought it from my dad after all."

"Were they trying to buy it?"

"He mentioned something about it the last time or two I spoke to him, but I never thought he'd sell."

"The title was transferred a few years after your mother died. The strange thing is, Doc didn't tell any of us about it. Mrs. Nash, she lost her husband years ago, had been paying rent all that time."

"Did she know she owned it? That husband of hers was a real Neanderthal, or so my mother called him. Buying that house without talking to her about it would fit the profile. The joke was on him if he died before he told her."

"Yes, I guess you're right. I never knew him, but she was a very sweet woman."

"Mom always liked her. She'd have been happy to know Angie, wasn't it? She'd have been happy to know Angie had her house."

She hung up and I sat on the rock, staring into space until Frank's voice broke through. "That must've been one doozy of a phone call."

I blinked and looked up at him. "I'm sorry. I've kept you standing in the cold, you must be freezing."

"And your lips are turning blue."

We started back and I filled Frank in on what Aggie had told me. "It would answer everything except for the fact that the title transferred after Mr. Nash died, so even if he bought it before he and his wife left that summer, Doc didn't get around to transferring title until he'd died."

"If she hadn't known about it, Doc coulda just kept the money and the house."

"Doc would never do that, Frank, for heaven sakes. Anyway, Mrs. Nash paid the property taxes every year since then so she obviously knew even though she paid rent to us when Doc stayed in our cabins, then she paid rent to the Tilamus after Doc died."

"And left the house to her granddaughter after she died."

"I wonder. Olivia told me her grandmother had recently changed the will." I stopped again and pulled out my cell.

"What?" asked Frank, but the line had already been answered.

"Mr. Clarke, it's Cara King in Coho Bay."

"Ms. King, thank you for sending the preliminary appraisal. It looks as though we'll have a buyer if Ms. Jordan decides to sell."

"Yes, Mr. Dickerson seems very interested. I wonder if you could tell me something."

"Yes?"

"Olivia told me that Mrs. Nash had recently changed her will. I'm wondering if she had originally left the house to the Tilamu heirs, Alex, Anne or Agatha."

"I'm not at liberty to reveal that."

"No, I didn't think you would be, but I'm not asking out of curiosity. Dan Simmons is investigating Mrs. Nash's death as a murder. As you're aware, we all thought the Tilamu heirs owned the house. Mrs. Nash paid rent as though they did and Alex brought Mr. Dickerson to Alaska in order to sell him the house, thinking his family owned it."

"Ms. King, I can assure you, the previous beneficiary was not related to Doctor Tilamu. I'm not aware of Mrs. Nash's actions in paying rent, but I can assure you there has never been any question in her mind that she is the legal owner of that property."

"Thank you, Mr. Clarke."

"I could have told you a lawyer will never tell you anything you really want to know," said Frank when I hung up the phone.

"He told me what matters. Mrs. Nash never doubted she owned the property and she never left it to the

Tilamus in her will. Alex wouldn't have killed her thinking he'd inherit from her and be able to go forward with the sale."

"Whose idiotic theory was that?"

"Mine, thank you very much. It seemed the only reason Mrs. Nash would pay rent was if she felt sorry for the Tilamus somehow. She didn't have any heirs, so I thought if she felt sorry for them, she might leave them the house."

"Shoots the heck outta that theory."

"Yes, but that's a good thing for Alex. If he killed her, it wouldn't have been premeditated."

"Unless he thought Mrs. Nash was lying."

"Lying?"

"When he confronted her and she told him she owned the house. If it were me, I wouldn't have taken a batty old woman's word for it, especially when she's been paying me rent every summer. I'd have thought she just didn't want me to sell it."

"But then why kill her? He wouldn't have thought she could stop him."

"That's my point."

We'd reached Mel's by then and I dropped onto the bench where we'd started and popped off my snowshoes. "I never thought of that. I just assumed he was mad because his dreams of all that money were being thwarted."

"You assume whatever people tell you is true. I don't and I don't think Alex seems like the type to take her word for it. He'd have wanted to check it out."

"Dickerson said that he waited at the marina but Alex didn't come, so he caught the ferry back instead. I can't imagine Alex would go to all the trouble of bringing the man out here, then leave him standing on the dock while he hustled into Juneau to check the title."

"No, but you're assuming Dickerson is telling the truth. Maybe he's the one who went to check on the title."

"And maybe he rented a boat in Juneau when he found out the old bat was telling the truth," said a voice behind Frank.

"Dan, you startled me. How long have you been standing there?"

"Long enough."

"Aggie called me back. She said she hasn't heard from Alex in years. Anne moved out to Washington State to take care of their brother after her husband died and she hasn't spoken with her since. Aggie blames her father for killing her mother by taking her back to Alaska instead of letting her stay in D.C. and go into a cancer hospital. She says she never forgave him for it and so she assumed he left the house to them and not her. When I told her Mrs. Nash owned the house, she mentioned the Nashes had wanted to buy the house, but she hadn't heard they actually did."

"Well, aren't you just a fount of information?"

"I am. Frank thinks Alex wouldn't have killed Mrs. Nash since there's no way he would have believed her."

"Unless he's just nuts," said Frank. "Some people can't control their temper."

"That's true. Some people can't." Dan looked intently at Frank, until Frank looked away.

"So what were you saying about Mr. Dickerson renting a boat?"

"I told you I was gonna check up on our great developer. Turns out he's under water."

"He's dead?"

Frank laughed. "He means he owes more than he owns."

"Not unheard of for a developer, but there are some properties he's gambled on that don't seem to be paying off. He needs a shot of cash pretty badly."

"But he wasn't selling, he was buying."

"He was offering Alex fifty thousand."

I whistled. "That's nothing. The land alone is worth four times that much."

"Which is where the shot of cash would come from. He'd grab it cheap then sell the land to shore up his cash flow."

"But that's not worth killing someone."

"It might be, if you stand to lose millions if you don't make that interest payment on time. That's the situation Dickerson is in."

"But by killing her, he ties the property up in escrow. If he were that hard up for cash, he'd walk away and look for another patsy."

"Which is why nobody kept his card," said Dan. "He was lowballing people, hoping they wouldn't know any better than Alex what their land was worth."

"So did he rent a boat and come back?" I asked.

"He rented a boat but he didn't have it out long enough to have come all the way back here."

"So if he didn't kill her and Alex didn't kill her then we're back to suicide?"

"Nope, we're very definitely thinking murder. The lab report came back. There were prints on the gun."

"Well, don't keep us in suspense, Dan."

"I called the prosecutor's office and they agreed I had enough for a warrant this time. They're contacting the Tacoma police."

"Alex? But we just eliminated him."

"You just eliminated him. I just eliminated Dickerson." Dan tipped his hat at me. "If you'll excuse me. Marcie invited me for dinner and I wouldn't want to be late."

Chapter 11

A week went by while we waited to see if the Tacoma police would arrest Alex. Dan told us they'd balked at the idea, but had finally agreed to cooperate and Dad had offered to take him up to Juneau to meet them at the airport. I chafed at being left behind. Even Frank had deserted me, claiming he needed to wrap a few things up at the mill.

"Caribou, if you're going to force me to rip out all of your stitches and do them over, I would prefer you didn't help."

"What? Oh. Sorry, Mom." I looked at the curtain she'd taken from me and was rapidly undoing the sewing I'd just done. "My mind's a million miles away."

"On a boat or at the mill?" asked Mel, smiling at me. She was sitting in her rocking chair, which Bent had moved to the family room and set beside the fireplace. Mom and I had been making curtains, but I was hopeless at sewing even when I was focused.

"Yes, dear, when are you planning on making a decision? You can't continue playing one against the other."

"I thought you told me I should play the field."

"I told you to explore your sexuality, which you seem determined not to do. If you must remain a virgin until marriage, then it's high time you choose one man or the other."

"Will everyone just stop talking about my sex life?"

"I would, if there were anything to stop talking about."

"Mother, stop teasing Cara. Now seriously, this town is too small for you to see both of them and I for one, think it's just too weird to keep having both of them here for dinner every night."

"And what's it going to be like if I do pick one, Mel? I can't exactly avoid the other."

"Nor can he avoid seeing you with the one you choose," Mom said, looking up from her sewing. "That is another good reason to choose soon, before either man is likely to be deeply hurt."

"What if I choose the wrong one?"

"What does your heart tell you, Cara?"

"Dan is very sweet and we can talk for hours. He's smart and funny."

"Then it's Daniel."

"Except that he's thirteen years older than I am and maybe someday that'll be nothing, but right now it seems huge. He's also, I'm not quite sure how to put it."

"Not anything near as sexy as Frank," said Mel.

"Well, yeah. I know, that's bad, but Frank is just, well, sexy."

Mom put her fabric down. "And what else?"

"He's funny. I don't know, Mom. What do you want me to say?"

"Are you in love with either of them, Cara?"

"I don't know. How did you know you loved Bent?"

Mel's face broke into a smile. "He's Bent. How could I not love him?"

"But how did you know?"

"It's difficult to put into words, Caribou. When you love a man, you just do. He's part of your life, part of your thoughts. You were perfectly fine before he came along and suddenly you realize you can't imagine life without him."

"You trust him, absolutely," added Mel. "You're completely honest with him, no games, no feeling like you have to be something you're not."

"But you want to be more than you are because of him."

"That makes no sense, Mom."

She smiled, a soft smile I didn't usually associate with my mother. "Love doesn't have to make sense. It just has to make you happy."

"What if I like both of them, but what if I'm not in love? If I choose now, and I choose the wrong one, I could realize after it's too late that I love the other one."

"Listen to your heart, Caribou. It will know when it's time to make a choice."

"But you both just said I have to choose now."

"We said you can't go on not choosing," said Mel, suppressing a giggle. "We didn't say you had to choose."

***

I don't know how word got out that my father and Dan were bringing Alex back for the murder of Mrs. Nash, but the whole town seemed to be at the marina when the boat pulled in. Fortunately the week had been warm and the snow was nothing more than puddles in the roadway. If it was going to be a normal winter, we'd have a few more nice weeks before the temperatures would drop consistently and the snow that fell would start hanging around. Being on the water, our winters were mild, with temperatures rarely falling lower than five or ten below and even that was only for short times. Today the thermometer outside Mel's had read forty-eight and as I looked around, I saw sweaters and sweatshirts but no coats.

Alex Tilamu, in contrast, looked like he'd dressed with the North Pole in mind. Granted, he'd been on the open water for three hours, but I didn't even own a coat with that much down in it. I tied off the boat for Dad to keep Dan's hands free to guide Alex up the ladder and onto the dock. I don't know what I'd expected from him, but whatever it was, I was disappointed. He didn't look like a murderer, but I suppose no one ever did.

I waited for the two men to get past me, then helped Dad close up the boat. "What do you think, Dad? Did he do it?"

"I really couldn't tell you, Kit. No one knows what evil hides in a person's mind."

"Wasn't that from an old radio show?"

"What? Oh, *The Shadow*. Close. I'm just glad Doc never lived to see this day."

I linked arms with him and we headed up the dock. There was an odd silence on the boardwalk, considering how many people were watching Dan and Alex making their way to City Hall. "Why did Dan bring him here, Dad? Wouldn't they hold him at Lemon Creek?" I asked, referring to the correctional facility in Juneau that houses both convicted felons and those awaiting trial.

"Dan said he had a slew of questions for him before he turns him over to the state. I don't think he'll break out, do you?" Dad nodded to a group of men who'd been standing in the street and who now took up positions around City Hall. Each man was carrying a rifle or shotgun and I knew each of them were former military.

"Bent?"

"Dan asked him to put together a rotating guard. He had to prove that we could be trusted to hang onto Alex before they agreed to let us take him. C'mon, Kit. I suspect there will be a few customers for Mel's tonight and she's only got your mother to help her cook."

"Heaven help us," I said, laughing and turning toward home. "Frank's on the second shift?"

"I don't know, honey. I wasn't here when Bent called out the troops."

"I just didn't see him, that's all. I'm sure he'll stop by."

"Is it Frank then?"

"Is what Frank?"

"Is he the one?"

"Dad, don't you start. I had a whole day of Mom and Mel's advice for the love-lorn."

He laughed. "Sorry. I don't think you could go wrong with either of them."

I waited. "But?"

"I like Dan. Always have. He's a good man."

"And Frank isn't?"

"I'm sure he is, honey. It's just that I've known Dan most of his life."

"You could say that in favor of any boy from the bay, Dad."

"That's true, and I'm sure you know Frank much better than any of us, so if he's good enough for you, Kit, he's good enough for me."

I stopped, pulling Dad onto a bench just shy of Mel's since the crowd was still concentrated on City Hall. "That's just it, Daddy. I don't know that I do know Frank. Dan talks to me, but Frank is just... There. He's funny and good-looking and he seems to be a good guy."

"Then why is he still in the running?"

"Because Dan kisses me and it's like I'm kissing my brother."

"You don't have a brother," Dad teased, "but I know what you mean, Kit. Sometimes you really like somebody but the spark isn't there."

"But sometimes the spark is a wildfire. That doesn't make it love, though does it?"

"So maybe you haven't met the right guy yet."

I leaned against his arm. "Mom thinks I haven't met the right woman."

"What?"

I laughed. "Never mind. We'd better get moving. People are starting to head this way and I don't want to have nothing but Mom's coffee to serve them."

"Or yours. Or mine for that matter. For Mel's sake, I hope her baby can cook."

***

The mood was subdued at Mel's that evening. Everybody had loved Doc and the thought that his only son had gone so wrong was disquieting. As I circulated, taking orders and refilling coffee cups, I listened to stories about Doc and Mrs. T. I'd mentioned to a few people what Aggie had told me about blaming her father and why, and that her mother had always been fond of Mrs. Nash. By the time I'd started serving pound cake, which was all Mom could bake that was actually edible, my gossip planting had reaped the desired effect. People who'd been on the fence about Mrs. Nash after Alex's outburst, were now sympathetic.

"Mom," I said, reporting in as she started washing dishes, "I give you three weeks to work on people after church and you'll be able to put together a delegation of residents asking Olivia to reconsider."

"I hope so, dear. Now, go help your father. Melody and I have things under control back here."

"That right, Melly?"

"Shoo, Cara. You baby me too much, all of you. I'm only pregnant. I'm not going to break with a little hard work."

"No morning sickness today?"

"No, thank goodness," answered my mother before Mel could. "She seems to be past that now."

"Nice to have you back, sis."

"Go, before Dad forgets himself and makes coffee."

I pushed through the door into the dining room and stopped cold. Dan was standing in the doorway, Alex beside him. Outside, I could see that two of the guard detail had stationed themselves on either side of the door. There was dead silence in the dining room. Even my Dad stood immobile, coffee pot poised over an empty cup.

"Dan, how can I help you?" My words sent ripples of whispers through the room.

"Penal code says I have to feed him," said Dan. "Thought I'd see if your mom could whip up something for him."

"That's cruel, Dan," said my father. There was scattered laughter. Everyone who had eaten tonight asked who was cooking before they ordered because they'd seen Bent guarding City Hall. "I'll see what Mel has left."

The uncomfortable silence descended again as soon as Dad left the room. "Dan, you two might be more comfortable in the kitchen." Dan looked around, as if seeing the crowd in the dining room for the first time. He nodded and pulled Alex with him through into the kitchen. I turned to the diners, friends, all of them. "Show's over, guys. Anybody need more food?" Silence, as people looked at each other, heads shaking. "Great. Finish your cake. Coffee's up here, help yourself. Leave money on the tables when you go. See you in church Sunday."

I dropped the dishtowel I'd picked up to wipe down the counter and headed for the kitchen. The murmurs behind me returned to an almost normal level. Alex was sitting on the stool Mel had vacated and Dan was leaning on the counter beside him, though I noticed he was far enough away Alex would have had a hard time grabbing his gun if he tried to lunge for it. Mom was staring at Alex while Mel was at the grill making burgers. Dad had gone to the back door to talk to the guards posted there.

"I'm done out there, Mel," I said, joining her at the grill. "Let me help."

"Fries," she said, nodding to where two baskets were bubbling in the hot oil.

I finished the fries while she built the burgers. I handed the plates to my mother, who put Dan's in front of him, but held Alex's. "Alexander Tilamu," she said, "you should be ashamed of yourself, asking my daughter to feed you after what you've done."

"Marcie," said Dan.

"No, I don't care, Daniel. Mrs. Nash was a friend of this family. What do you have to say for yourself, Alexander?" She emphasized each word with a wave of the plate. My dad caught it on 'say' and slid it over to Alex. She glared at him before finishing her sentence.

"Marcie, you can't ask a person questions when he's in police custody."

"Why not, Robert? I want to hear directly from him what was so important that he would take the life of a gentle, loving woman who was never anything but his mother's friend and a companion to his father during his grief. Tell me that, Alexander Tilamu."

Alex hadn't looked up even once as my mother ranted. His hands rested on the table, his food untouched. Mel and I exchanged looks, holding our breaths to hear what he would say. Judging from how loudly my mother had voiced her demand, I'd guess most of the folks in the dining room beyond were wondering if Alex would give her an answer.

"I don't know what to say, Mrs. King," Alex said at last, disappointing the dining room because I could barely hear him and I was standing four feet from him. He pushed his plate away. "Dan, I'm not hungry."

"I'll box it up," I said, mostly because I couldn't stand to not be doing anything. I pulled down two boxes, because Dan hadn't had a chance to eat either, and after looking at Dan, gave them both to Alex, who nodded his thanks.

"Where are they?" A woman's voice, high pitched and bordering on hysterical, flooded in from the dining room.

"Don't let her in here!" shouted Alex. Dan put a hand on his gun and I stepped protectively in front of Mel, who slapped my shoulder and told me to stop blocking her view.

A tall, well-dressed woman burst into the kitchen, the guard from the front of the restaurant hurrying in behind her along with a sizable number of the people who'd been left in the dining room when I'd gone into the kitchen. At least, the few who could fit pushed into the kitchen. The rest pressed against the door like the crowd at a rock concert trying to see the band after the show.

"Elizabeth Anne Buchanan," said my mother, using the same voice she used when Mel or I were in big trouble, "what are you doing shoving your way into my daughter's kitchen?"

"Don't you talk to me like that Marcia King," she answered. "Your daughter works for me, don't forget. I'll go anywhere I please."

"Yes, let's talk about that, Elizabeth."

"It's Anne!"

"You have been collecting rent fraudulently ever since your father died. What do you have to say about that?"

"Marcie!" Dan tried, but he'd have as much luck standing between two charging moose and persuading them to turn around.

"I've been doing no such thing," Anne replied. "I don't care what any piece of paper says, that house is ours. My father built that house for my mother, not some hussy who murdered her husband to get her hooks into him."

This set off a lot of talk in the crowd beyond the kitchen doors so I came to Mrs. Nash's defense. "She never killed anyone, Anne. Your father sold her the house because she loved it and you didn't."

"What do you know about it?"

"I know that every time I called you or your brother, asking you—begging you these past few years—to let me fix what was broken, you said you didn't care. All you ever cared about was the money and that's all you care about now." I turned my attention to Alex. He was sitting with his head on the table, his arms over his head as if to shield himself from his sister's words. "You killed her for nothing, Alex. You killed that beautiful old woman and you'll never get a dime because that house was never, ever yours."

"That's enough!" Dan's voice broke through the collective noise of the assembled crowd. "Go home, all of you, do you hear me? Go home!"

He signaled the guards and except for Bent, who'd come in from the back door when he heard Anne shouting, they herded the townspeople out of the kitchen. I heard the bell chiming in the dining room as the room cleared. There was a silent hostility in the kitchen, broken only by Alex, who seemed to be sobbing or choking, I couldn't tell which. Mom and

Anne stood glaring at each other, while Mel and I huddled on the far side of the room. Dad stood with Bent near the door, my brother-in-law with the steely stare on his face I'd only seen once before.

When the chimes finally stopped, Dan looked at those of us who were left. "I am not, repeat not, going to try this case in public."

"There isn't any case," said Anne, her voice straining with the effort to control it. "My brother did not kill that woman."

"That's enough, Anne." Alex's voice was weak and she ignored him.

"You're responsible for this," Anne said, turning on Dan. "By the time my lawyer gets through with you, you'll wish you'd never been born."

"Here's my card," said Dan, holding it out to her, "have him give me a call."

Anne slapped the card away from him. "Come, Alex. We're getting out of this two bit town." She pulled his arm.

Bent stepped up to her, his shotgun in a ready pose. "Step away from him, ma'am."

Anne tugged at Alex, who pulled his arm out of her grasp. "Stop it, Anne. This isn't one of your stupid community theater shows." He held his hands up to her, wrists together as though he were wearing handcuffs. "I'm under arrest. For murder."

She took a step back, stunned by her brother's outburst. "That's... that's ridiculous. My attorney—"

"Dumped you because you couldn't pay his bills. Don't you think I already called him? Just get out of here, Anne. Dan, get me out of here." He shoved past his sister and went to stand by the door. Bent opened the door for Alex and, along with the guard who'd remained outside, escorted Alex out.

The door banged shut behind them, setting Anne off on a tear jag. "It's all your fault," she choked out as she sobbed. I wasn't sure who she was talking to, but from the look on my mother's face, I didn't think she cared.

"Anne, do you have a place to stay while you're in Coho Bay?" I asked, trying to diffuse the situation.

"Caribou, what are you saying?"

"Mom, it's too dark for her to head back to Juneau tonight."

"I don't care if she sleeps in her boat. I don't care if she sleeps on a bench on the boardwalk. She is not setting foot inside any property owned by this family." She turned to look at Anne, who was still sobbing. "That includes this property. Daniel, please escort this trespasser out. There. Charge her with trespassing and she can sleep in the cell next to her brother."

"We only have one cell, Marcie," said Dan and if I didn't know him better, I'd say he was trying not to laugh.

"Well, that'll be cozy then. Just get her out of here." Mom went past my dumb-struck father and stomped her way up the stairs.

"You need me, Dan?" asked Dad. Dan shook his head. "I'd better go see if I can calm her down, though I can't really say she said anything I wasn't thinking."

I looked at my dad in surprise, but he just winked at me and headed up the stairs. "Mel, you go up too. I'll finish up here."

"Are you sure?"

"It's just dishes. I'll be up in half an hour."

"All right. Dan, don't let Bent stand guard duty all night."

"He doesn't listen to me either, Mel, but I'll try."

She went upstairs and Dan and I stared at Anne Buchanan, who had continued to sniffle while my family had said their good-byes. "Why all the drama, Anne?" I asked once I was sure Mel was out of earshot.

"It may be drama to you, Cara, but it is terribly real to me. How would you feel if someone accused your brother of murder?"

"I'm sure it must be upsetting for you, but barging in here causing a scene isn't doing Alex any good." She sat on the stool. Dan took a step back, nodding at me to continue. "You must have been shocked to find out the title on the house had changed. I know I was."

"Shocked isn't the word for it."

"Did you ever wonder why you weren't contacted by the probate attorney when your father died?"

"I did wonder, but I assumed my father had left the house to Aggie. She's the oldest and she was always," her voice cracked. *Genuinely, this time*, I thought. "She was always his favorite. Whenever they came down to visit, they'd always go to Aggie's house. Alex and I had to go there if we wanted to see our parents."

"That must have galled you."

"It was inconvenient, that's all. I went, of course, when Aggie called and told me mother was ill. We tried to convince daddy to let her stay in D.C. and go to a real hospital. Aggie was convinced it would have saved her, but daddy told us mother wanted to go home. Aggie was devastated when mother died. She was so angry, she refused to go to the funeral."

"What about you? Were you angry?"

"Not then."

"You came then? To your mother's funeral." She looked sharply at me. "I was a kid. I don't remember the funeral."

She hesitated. "I wasn't able to come. I wanted to, of course, but I just wasn't able to make it."

"My parents were happy to see you last week, after Mrs. Nash died. They hoped you or Alex might want to move back here."

"Ha! This place," she gestured at the kitchen as though it represented all of Coho Bay, "may be enough for you, but it's hardly big enough to keep a fly busy. I prefer Seattle."

"Alex stayed over, but I didn't see you the next day at the funeral."

"I took a walk. It didn't take long to remind me what I hated about this place so I told Alex he could find his own way home when he was ready. I took the ferry back to Juneau and flew home."

"Why would Alex say Mrs. Nash killed your mother?"

She looked at me, then down at her hands. "When we heard about the house, I was angry. I may have said something like that."

"But you don't really think that."

"There had to be some reason Daddy would cut his own children out of his will in favor of that woman. I looked her up. Her husband died the year Mama did. Some freak accident. It sounded fishy to me."

"But they never married. They were friends, that's all."

"On Daddy's part, maybe. Maybe it sickened him to think she'd kill to be with him."

"Anne," I put my hand on her arm, "I was old enough to remember Doc and the summers when he and Mrs. Nash were both here. They were friends. She didn't kill anyone."

She looked at my hand and when she looked up at me, the hate in her eyes was like a slap. I pulled back as though I'd been touching a flame. "You're wrong."

"Come on, Mrs. Buchanan," said Dan, "let's see if I can find you a place to sleep tonight and we'll get this worked out in the morning."

She stood up and straightened herself. Though she came only to eye level with him, she seemed to be staring down at him. "I am fifty-eight years old, Daniel Simmons. I'm quite capable of finding my own way in the world." She marched through the doors to the dining room. I followed as far as the counter. As she reached the front door, she turned to look at me and again her eyes held a look of pure hatred. "You'll be sorry you ever crossed my family, Cara King."

I didn't know I was shaking until Dan put his hand on the small of my back. "Don't let her scare you," he whispered.

"I don't get it, Dan. She's a hissing, snarling tiger, then she sobs and plays the loving sister, then suddenly she's looking daggers at me. I don't get it."

"I think I do."

I turned and found his arms around me reassuring. "What?"

"I'm not sure yet. There's something going on here that doesn't sit right, but I don't think you're in danger."

"Not with Dad and Bent around."

"And me." There was something in his tone and when he leaned down to kiss me it sparked.

Chapter 12

I couldn't sleep. I suppose, all things considered, that shouldn't have been a shock but when I finally gave up staring at the ceiling and went downstairs, the fact that it was two in the morning came as a surprise. Bent had come home at midnight. I'd heard him and poked my head out of my little guest room to see whether anything exciting had happened after he'd taken Alex away.

"Not a thing, little sister," he'd answered, keeping his voice down to avoid waking the others.

"Did Anne go see him?"

"She's camped out in the lobby, sleeping on that nasty couch."

"Seriously?"

"She wanted to sleep in the cell with Alex, but Frank told her to get over herself."

"Frank was there?"

"He's standing guard until two, then Chuck's taking over until Dan comes in. Practically had to carry him outta there to get him to go home. Man needs to sleep once in a while."

"So do you."

"My thoughts exactly," he said, disappearing into the bedroom he shared with Mel.

Now, standing in the kitchen, I stared at the number on the clock and decided to go find Frank. I'm not entirely sure why I decided to go, but I found myself a short time later standing in front of the gallery, watching Frank leave City Hall and cross the road.

"What are you doing here, Cara? You'll catch your death of cold."

"Been there, done that," I joked. It wasn't much of a joke, but it kept my teeth from chattering. "I couldn't sleep."

"So you climbed out of a warm bed to come stand in front of City Hall on the off chance I'd be coming out right about now?"

"Bent told me you'd be getting off at two."

The grin spread slowly across his face. "Might that be why you couldn't sleep?"

It was a good thing it was too dark for him to see me blush. "I couldn't stop thinking about the Tilamus. This whole thing is crazy."

"Let's continue this discussion upstairs, before you turn into an icicle." He led me around the building and I waited while he unlocked the door. Considering it was my own apartment, it was a strange feeling. "I heard about Anne."

"It was crazy, Frank. I get that she didn't want him to talk without an attorney and my mother really was out of line going after Alex like that."

"I heard she was scary-good."

I laughed. "She really was. I thought Dan was gonna have a stroke when she asked him why he killed Mrs. Nash. Would have been nice if Alex had the guts to have told her."

"Couldn't have gotten a word in edgewise with his sister there, is what I heard." Frank pulled a beer from the fridge and offered me one, but I shook my head.

"She was even worse than Mom. Every minute a different mood. If you don't like this Anne, wait ten minutes and you'll get the next."

"Did you learn anything?"

"Her sister Aggie thought they got the house and they thought Aggie did, and since the two sides weren't talking to each other, nobody put two and two together. When I started sending Alex and Anne the rent money, they just shut up and took it."

"Nice family."

"But why on earth did Alex think he could get away with selling it? He hadn't spoken to Aggie in years. How was he going to get her to sign off on it?"

"Maybe Anne was going to sign it for her."

"I hadn't thought of that. She'd have to fake an ID, but I guess that wouldn't be too hard."

"Is she the type?"

"I wouldn't put it past her."

"So the question becomes when did they find out Aggie didn't own the property? If we believe Dickerson, it was when he and Alex showed up at the end of the season."

"You already pointed out that Alex wouldn't have taken her word for it. He'd check the title records."

"Then he'd have to discredit Mrs. Nash. Accuse her of getting the property as part of an illegal transaction so he could get it back or maybe intimidate Olivia into giving him the property outright. She is a soft-hearted kind of woman."

Something stirred in the back of my mind at the hint of wistfulness in Frank's tone when he mentioned Olivia but I pushed it away. "Alex wouldn't have known what kind of person Olivia was and the idea of accusing Mrs. Nash of murder in order to get the house back is pretty crazy."

"Crazy sounds like the sister. Maybe she put him up to it."

"She's crazy, but I don't think she's stupid and that was flat out stupid on Alex's part even just being here and drawing attention to himself." I sat on the arm of the couch. "Something just doesn't sit right."

***

Frank walked me back to Mel's and I finally managed to fall asleep but I couldn't have been in bed longer than a couple of hours before Mom shook me awake again. "Caribou, wake up." I moaned, not wanting to get out of my bed. "There's something going on at City Hall."

That woke me up. "What is it? Is Dan okay?"

"I have no idea. I only know the whole town's up in arms again." She let go of me and went to the door. "Get dressed. Bent and your father are already gone."

With incentive like that, I out of bed and was in front of City Hall in ten minutes. I don't usually consider it an advantage to be unusually tall. I'd spent much of my life hunched over, trying not to tower over everyone around me, but today being tall was a gift because I was five people back in the crowd. My mother was hopping from one foot to the other, but all she could see were the backs of people's shoulders. "What's happening, Caribou?"

"I don't know, Mom. The guards are keeping people outside."

"Nonsense! This is the people's house." She elbowed through the crowd like an offensive lineman leading his running back into the end zone. Remembering my high school quarterback days, I wasted no time following her.

"Mrs. K, I can't let you in."

"Donald Lighthorse, stand aside or I'll take you over my knee like I did when I used to babysit you." Poor Donny bore the brunt of laughs from the crowd like a trooper, but when my mother puts her mind to something, it's best not to be in her way. She turned and led the crowd in a chant. "This is the people's house! This is the people's house!" There was a sudden surge from behind me and I found myself propelled into the lobby, throwing my arms out in an unsuccessful attempt to stay upright.

Thankfully, Donny doesn't hold a grudge. He pulled me to my feet before the wave could flatten me and I found myself face to face with a very angry Anne Buchanan. "You again!" she screamed. Her face looked like a radish from Mom's garden and there was a dribble of spit cresting the corner of her lip. Her eyes had narrowed when she saw me and she jabbed at me with a bony finger as she spoke.

I tried to step back, but I was hemmed in by the throng behind me. Anne grabbed my arm, pulling me forward and twisting it behind my back. She spun me around, placing my body between hers and an equally angry Dan. The scene had a disturbingly theatrical quality, though there was nothing imaginary about the pain in my arm.

Her voice was shrill. "Let him go, Dan Simmons, or I'm gonna break your little girlfriend's arm."

The woman was more than twice my age but she was tall, had twenty pounds more muscle and the hands that gripped me were strengthened by desperation. I wasn't sure whether to be scared or embarrassed by the fact that I wasn't able to shake her off. I have got to start working out.

Alex shouted at her from his cell, "You're not helping me! Don't be such a drama queen, Anne!"

She screamed at him. "Shut up! If you were able stay sober longer than ten minutes you wouldn't be in that cell." She kept yanking my arm until I thought she was going to pull it out of the socket. I hoped the little whimpering cries I was hearing were coming from somebody else. It was bad enough to get my arm ripped off by an old woman, I had to go and do it in front of the whole town. I was never going to live this down.

"Elizabeth Anne Buchanan, take your hands off my daughter this instant!"

Mom's voice cut through the insanity, as harsh and effective as a slap in the face. For a moment Anne wavered, but she must have caught the violent look in Mom's eyes because she shoved me at Dan, sending both of us to the floor.

She drew herself up to her full height, towering over my mother. "My name," she said through clenched teeth, "is Anne."

"For crying out loud," I hissed into Dan's ear, "that's what she's gonna get upset about?"

"Call yourself the Queen of England, for all I care," my mother responded. "If you touch my child again, I will kill you with my bare hands."

A cheer went up from the crowd and Anne literally shook with her anger. Her hands clenched into fists, but she couldn't intimidate my mother. My mom may drive me crazy sometimes, but nobody threatens one of her kids. She's like a she-bear protecting her cub when it comes to Mel and me.

Anne took a step away from Mom, then dropped her voice and raised her chin. "I am too much of a lady to say what I think of you, Marcia King."

"Well, I'm too much of a lady not to say exactly what I think of you," retorted my mother.

"You tell her, Mrs. K," shouted Donny Lighthorse, drawing a glare from Anne.

"You just you watch yourself," she said, trying to twist her lip into a snarl, but it was hard to take her seriously now that my arm was speaking to me again.

"Is that a threat?" My mother took a step toward the older woman and a chill ran through me at the shift in her tone. I nudged Dan, who had been leaning back on his hands, enjoying the show.

He sighed and scrambled to his feet, pulling me up after him. "I'll take it from here, Marcie." My mother took the tiniest possible step back and Dan turned to Anne. "Back off." She didn't budge. "Do you want me to arrest you for assault?"

"Do it, Dan!" shouted a man from the doorway.

"You're not helping, Earl," Dan said without taking his eyes off her. "What's it gonna be, Mrs. Buchanan?"

She stammered, looking around for some show of support. There wasn't a friendly face in the room, but she stuck out her chin and stood her ground. "You can't keep me from seeing my brother."

"I don't want to see her."

She wheeled on her brother, striding to the door of his cell. "Shut up, Alex. I'm trying to help."

He retreated as best he could. "I don't need your help."

"You tell, her, Alex."

"Earl!" yelled Dan, but the fisherman, getting back slaps from his buddies, only grinned at him. Dan turned his attention back to Anne, who was gripping the bars as though she thought she could bend them open. "You want to help him, get out of here and go get him a good lawyer. You can see him again when he gets to Lemon Creek."

Anne shook the bars, rattling the door but accomplishing little else. Her shoulders sagged for a moment, then she straightened, releasing her grip. Alex remained pressed against the far wall, out of range should she suddenly decide to reach her arm through. Her voice was controlled, cold. "You're on your own. Do you hear me? I wash my hands of you. I should have listened to Aggie and cut you off years ago. You don't want my help? Fine. You can rot in prison in this God-forsaken state for the rest of your life for all I care. I'm done."

"Good," said Alex. His voice was defiant, but I noticed he didn't get any closer to her. "With your crappy lawyer, I'd probably get the chair."

Anne's back stiffened. Without saying another word, she marched out of the building. I would have felt sympathy for her if my shoulder wasn't constantly reminding me why I shouldn't. She wasn't a woman you'd want to cross, but neither was my mother. I wondered if I'd ever been as ungrateful for my mother's help as Alex was for Anne's. I threw my arms around my mother, ignoring the pain, thankful to have her on my side.

"Okay, folks," said Dan, breaking the silence that had accompanied Anne's retreat. "Show's over. Everybody can clear out now." He and his crew of volunteer guards started herding the crowd out onto the road.

I knew they'd head to Mel's and she was going to need help with them. I gave her another squeeze. "You'd better head back to the restaurant."

There was a glistening of tears in her eyes, emotion I'd rarely seen, but she just patted my cheek. "Don't be too long." She slipped away with the last of the townsfolk and suddenly, it was just Alex and me in a quiet lobby.

"Is she gone?" His voice sounded small inside the cell.

"Everybody's gone."

"She's a witch."

I crossed to the cell door and looked in at him. What a pitiful lump of a man to have killed such a sweet old woman. "She's not my favorite person either, but she was trying to help."

"You see where her help has gotten me."

"You're blaming your sister for what you did?"

"I didn't do anything." His voice carried a whiff of temper tantrum. "If she hadn't introduced me to that developer, I never would have been there when the old bat shot herself."

I bit back a retort and tried to stay focused. "Anne introduced you to Dickerson?"

"She met him at some hoity-toity function in Seattle. She likes to get all dressed up and pretend to be somebody." He spit on the floor of the cell. "He'd been looking for property in Alaska, something run-down that he could flip for a profit."

"But she knew she didn't own the house."

He shrugged. "Aggie'd never taken an interest in the house so why should she profit from it? My job was show him the house and get him to make an offer. Anne said she'd take care of the rest."

"By forging Agatha's name? That's a felony."

"Only if Aggie reported it. She wouldn't have done that even if she'd found out about it. I told you, she didn't care and she sure doesn't need the money." He laid back on the narrow cot and stared up at the ceiling, arms crossed behind his head.

"So you brought Dickerson up to see the house."

"He loved it. Loved the town, the cruise ship trade. Loved the mountains and the setting right on the bay like that. Heck, he'd have made a killing on that house. I told Anne we should double the price."

"Anne was there?"

He went on as though he hadn't heard me. "And then that Nash bat goes and says she owns it. Told us she'd owned it for years."

"But you didn't believe her."

"I thought she was blowing smoke to keep us from selling the house, though why she wanted to live there is beyond me. That place is a dump. You know, you've really done a crappy job of taking care of the place."

It was my turn to grip the bars and rattle the door, but I didn't tell him what I thought of his opinion. I wanted to hear him admit to killing Mrs. Nash. "What did you do when she insisted she owned the house?"

He sat up, swinging his legs over the side of the cot. "What could I do? Anne would've killed me if I let this sale fall through. I told Dickerson to take a walk. I tried to talk to her, but she just kept laughing at me and telling me what a disappointment I would have been to my father."

"That must have made you angry."

"Angry doesn't mean I killed her. Why should I? I thought she was lying. I told her she wouldn't pay us rent all those years if she owned the house."

"I've been wondering about that myself."

"She said she did it to protect our father's reputation, that he hadn't wanted anybody to know he'd disowned his kids." He ran his hand over the stubble on his face. "Told me to look up the deed for myself if I didn't believe her then she told me to get out."

Red spots appeared on his cheeks and I wondered if their conversation had made him angry enough to kill. "I would have been furious."

"I told you. She threw me out. I went looking for Anne."

Again, his insistence that Anne had been in Coho Bay that day. "Did she come down on the boat with you?"

He shook his head. "She didn't want to overwhelm Dickerson. She came on the ferry."

"Why?"

"Because she didn't trust me not to screw it up."

"What did she say when you found her?"

"I didn't find her." He sat up, swinging his legs over the side of the bed. "She said she'd be waiting on the trail if I needed her. I figured she must've seen Dickerson leave and took off after him."

"I'm confused. If you left, and Mrs. Nash was alive enough to ask you to leave—"

"She was, I swear it."

"Then why did you go back?"

"Because I left my coat there."

"You what?" I wasn't sure what I'd been expecting him to say, but I knew that wasn't it. Dan hadn't mentioned anything about finding a man's coat in the house.

"I left my damned coat in the damned living room and I went back to get it." Alex punctuated each profanity by slapping his hand against the side of his head. "When I got there, there was blood all over it. I grabbed it and the gun fell. I picked it up!" Much as I hated to admit it, his voice had a ring of truth. Either that or he was a very good liar. "I'm an idiot. Anne's told me a million times, but my God ... the old dame was sittin' there, head blown half off. I just dropped everything and ran." He went back to slapping his head.

I shuddered, remembering how I'd felt walking into that room and her death had happened weeks before I got there. I didn't want to think about what it would have been like on the day she died. "Why did you show up at her funeral? Why come back at all since nobody knew you'd been here?"

"I left my coat there. I couldn't remember if there was anything in the pockets that would link it to me. Anne told me to stay on the boat and she'd go talk to the cops to find out what they knew."

Why would he lie about something so easily disproven? It was true Anne had been there that day because my parents saw her, but Dan would have mentioned if she'd gone to City Hall. "Why draw attention to yourself by making a scene at the funeral?"

"You ever spend three hours on a boat with Anne telling you what a jerk you are? I was drunk outta my head. I don't even remember being there." He got up, grabbing one of the bars to stay on his feet and I took a step back. "Look, what's it matter? I'm dead. I've never had nothing but bad luck my whole life. We shoulda bull-dozed that house years ago."

"Cry me a river, Tilamu." Dan came up behind me and slid his arm around my waist. "Don't listen to his sob stories, Cara."

"I'm telling you, Simmons, that woman was already dead."

"Tell it to the judge." Dan pulled me away from the cell door. "You'd better get over to Mel's. The whole town's turned out for this."

"What about him?" I asked, nodding toward Alex.

"He ain't hungry."

"No, I meant what he said about Anne."

"I didn't do it."

"Zip it, Tilamu." Dan shook his head. "Perps tell all kinds of stories, Cara. There's no evidence Mrs. Buchanan was anywhere near Coho Bay when Mrs. Nash was killed and there was no coat in the house."

"Yes, but—"

I rubbed my shoulder. I wasn't satisfied, but Dan knew more about these things than I did, even if he'd only been a beat cop in Fairbanks. "Where's Anne now?"

"I don't know and I don't care as long as she isn't here." He gave me a quick kiss then pushed me toward the door. "Save me some coffee."

The sun had risen while I'd been inside and was casting a thin golden light on the town giving the buildings an eerie quality. Though I'd help lay every log and drive every nail in it, my gallery looked foreign. I leaned on a post and tried to persuade myself to go help feed the hoards. I took a few steps, but it wasn't until my feet hit the mud and gravel path leading to the residential area that I realized I wasn't headed to the restaurant.

I found myself on the doorstep of the Tilamu house, reaching into the mailbox. Dan had been in and out of the house so many times, it had been simpler to keep the key on site than for him to come and find me every time he needed access. I supposed I should take it back now. I unlocked the door and dropped the key in my pocket as I walked in. It felt like an eternity since I'd found Mrs. Nash's body.

I shrugged off my coat and laid it on the counter. I avoided looking at the living room. I hoped Olivia would tear the house down, if only because I didn't want to clean that room. I walked through the two larger bedrooms, then into the small bedroom that would have belonged to Alex, not sure what I was looking for. His bitterness about his family had shaken me. I'd liked Doc and it seemed like a betrayal to think of him as anything other than a loving father.

The closet door was standing open and I went to close it, not that it mattered but for some reason it annoyed me. Glancing up, I noticed an attic access panel, shoved off to one side, leaving an opening a few inches wide. The crime lab must have been very thorough to have searched the attic and I stood on my toes, trying to move it back into place but my fingers only skimmed the surface. I'd need something to climb on, but the room held only a bed and dresser. Cursing the compulsion that was driving me to straighten up a house that would likely be torn down, I went to get a chair from the dining area. A moment later, I felt something crash into the back of my head. I staggered, throwing out my arms to catch myself but someone shoved me hard in the back and I fell forward. My head, already stinging from the first blow, thudded against the wall.

I saw stars. Collapsing onto the floor, my back to the wall, I tried to focus my eyes on my attacker. Dimly, I registered danger, but my mind was too foggy to force my body into motion. "Anne? What are you doing here?"

"What are you doing in my house?"

"It's not your house." I gingerly fingered my head, relieved I didn't find any blood since my head was still swimming. "What were you thinking hitting me like that? You could have killed me."

"What are you do snooping around my house?" There was a manic edge to her voice that was setting off alarm bells loud enough it's a wonder she didn't hear them.

I did my best to keep my voice calmer than I was. "You shouldn't be here, Anne." I grabbed a chair and pulled myself up slowly, fighting back the urge to throw up. "You need to leave."

"No one is driving me out of my house." She lowered the volume of her voice and while the effect was menacing, the throbbing in my head appreciated the quiet.

"Your father sold this house to Mrs. Nash years ago. I looked up the title. It belongs to her granddaughter now."

"This house belongs to my family. It always has and it always will."

I straightened and was happy to find the world remained roughly where I expected it to be. I held onto the back of the chair just in case. "Cut the crap, Anne. You were going to sell it."

She didn't answer and I saw a flicker of something like uncertainty in her eyes. I wanted to bolt but she had positioned herself between me and the door. I picked up a chair, ready to use it as a weapon if needed, and went back into the bedroom, closing and locking the door behind me. I crossed to the window, but it had been nailed shut. Dad and I had done that because Mrs. Nash had been paranoid about bears. I'd tried to tell her a bear wasn't going to open a window to get in, but she'd pestered me until I gave up and nailed all the windows except the one in her bedroom shut.

Anne was pounding on the door and I didn't want to be standing there with nothing but a chair to defend myself with if she managed to get in. My head ached and I would have given anything to be able to lay down on the bed until the room stopped spinning. The pounding got worse. Anne must have found something to use as a battering ram. Panicked, I dragged the chair into the closet and climbed up, shoving the access panel out of the way. Light from the bad roof filtered into the attic and for the first time, I was happy the Tilamus hadn't let me repair it. I looked around at the empty space, hoping all the spiders had died with the cold weather, wondering if I could punch a hole through the roof and get out that way before Anne realized I was gone.

A pile of cloth caught my eye and I reached for it, but it was just out of my grasp. I adjusted myself on the chair, lifting up on my toes, putting one foot on the back of the chair to give me a few extra inches. As my fingers connected with the cloth, my feet lost contact with the chair. Before I could catch myself, I fell, hitting the solid frame around the access panel.

***

I woke to pitch dark. I hadn't thought I'd been out long enough for morning to become night, but there wasn't a hint of light around me. I was laying on my side, my face flat on what felt like a wooden floor. The closet. I remembered climbing on the chair and feeling it slip from under me. I started to sit up but a blinding pain in my shoulder stopped me. I'd broken my collar bone during a football game once and I was pretty sure I'd broken it again. Add that to the increasingly large lump on my head and I was wishing I'd gone to help Mel instead of heading for the Tilamu house. The sound of voices cut through my self-pity.

"What are you doing here? I told you I'd take care of this." It was Anne. She was in the bedroom, but who was she talking to? I couldn't hear the reply, but whatever the person said, it must have made her angry. "I had to! That coat has my blood on it and that freak woman was in the closet when I got here. Ten more seconds and she would have found it."

Alex's coat! Of course, that's what the cloth must have been. Alex said he dropped the coat and ran after finding Mrs. Nash's body but why would Anne's blood be on it and how had it gotten into the attic? I could hear a voice answering her, but again, I couldn't make out what was said. Had Alex broken out of jail? Had he hurt Dan doing it? I had to get to him. I pulled my injured arm against my side and rolled over, leveraging myself up with my good arm. I sat for a moment, eyes closed since I couldn't see anyway, breathing deeply until the pain ebbed. I heard them talking, though both voices were too quiet to distinguish who was saying what.

I was desperately afraid they'd stop arguing long enough to remember I was here and I was relieved when I heard a door slam. Before I could move, I heard footsteps and another noise, something like water splashing out of a bucket. The smell of gasoline hit me and I scrambled to my feet, as quickly as I could with only one good arm. Playing possum in a pitch dark closet wasn't going to be a good strategy if they set the house on fire with me in it. If I had to fight my way out, I couldn't have worse odds than if I stayed put. I put my hand on the doorknob and turned.

It was locked. Who puts a lock on a closet door? I went through a litany of things I planned to say to Alex Tilamu when I saw him again, but first I had to get out of that closet. I could smell smoke now, making my heart race. I was pretty sure they wouldn't stick around once the fire was set and even if they did, I'd rather take my chances with a crazy old woman and her mystery man than die locked in a closet.

I thought about the day Coach had taught me how to tackle, and threw my good shoulder against the closet door. If you've never slammed into a locked door with a broken collar bone, no matter which shoulder you're using, I don't recommend it. The pain took my breath away and I would have cried if I weren't so desperate to get out. I pushed my back against the wall and pulled my leg up to my chin, kicking out at the door as hard as I could. My foot broke through the panel and my body slammed against the door again, but the lock held. I started to pull my leg back but shards of wood grabbed my thigh, trapping me. It seemed like a good time to panic and that's exactly what I did, pounding on the door and screaming for help.

I heard my father's voice somewhere outside the house. It was so distant I wasn't sure if my mind was playing tricks on me but I didn't care. If his voice was a hallucination, I was going with it. "Daddy! Daddy, help me!" I shouted, but no one answered. The smoke was thick, flowing into the closet from the jagged opening around my leg. I pulled my shirt up over my nose and mouth and struggled with the broken panel, pounding the area around my thigh, trying to widen the opening enough so I could free my leg. I cried out in frustration, unable to budge it.

"She's here!" a voice boomed on the other side of the closet door.

He sounded like an angel and I wondered again if I were imagining it, but again, I didn't care. "Frank? Frank, my leg's stuck in the door and I can't get it out. The door's locked. I tried to kick it open."

"Hang on." I felt his fingers slip into the hole around my thigh. He broke enough of the shards for me to retrieve my leg. I was still stuck in a smoke-filled closet but at least I wasn't going to die with my leg dangling through a closet door. I don't know why that thought comforted me, but I'm ashamed to say it did. "Move out of the way, Cara."

I tripped over the chair in the darkness, falling backwards at least what I imagined was far enough from the door to avoid Frank when he crashed through. I reached out with my good arm and he pulled me up. I tried to thank him, but the noise of the fire was deafening. He half-carried, half-dragged me to the window which someone had managed to smash and I almost fell out of it into my father's arms. Smoke billowed through the opening as Frank climbed out and the two of them carried me away from the house.

Townsfolk were watching members of the volunteer fire department pump water from a thousand gallon tank mounted on the back of a flatbed truck. I stood between my father and Frank, both still having to hold me up in order to keep me from falling, and stared open-mouthed at the house. Judging by the flames shooting through the roof, I suspected Olivia wouldn't have to decide whether tear the house down or try to restore it. I watched in stunned silence, shivering until Frank put his coat over my shoulders. I looked up at him, blinking back tears. "You saved my life."

He winced, looking suddenly uncomfortable. "Anybody would've done the same."

"You went into a burning building to save me."

"How did you know Cara was in there?" Dad asked. "I heard the bell, but by the time I got here, you were already in the house."

"I was standing in my apartment, looking out at the bay and saw Cara head over here. When that nutball woman took off after her, I thought I'd better get dressed and see what was going on."

"Are you talking about Anne Buchanan?" asked my mother, who'd joined us and was trying to find a way to hug me without it hurting.

"Anne hit me over the head with a vase, then she locked me in the closet and set fire to the house."

"She did what?" My mother looked as stunned as I'd felt.

Frank nodded, relinquishing his place beside me. "That's where she was when I found her."

"Oh, my stars." Mom was crying as she kissed my cheek, then her voice hardened. "I am going to kill that woman."

"Now, Marcie. Let the law deal with her." Dad shook as the surge of adrenalin began to wear off. "I didn't know you were in there, Kit, until Frank handed you to me out the window." He kissed the top of my head. I winced, but I didn't mind. At least pain meant I was still alive. "I've never been so scared in all my life."

I leaned my head gently against his chin. "Me too, Daddy."

"You look positively frightful." Mom was poking at the rips in my jeans, which were soaked with blood from where the door had dug into my skin.

"Ouch, Mom. Cut that out."

Her eyes softened. "I'm sorry. I didn't mean to sound so harsh." She put her hand on the back of my head and showed me the blood on her fingers. "We've got to get you to a doctor. Robert?"

"Heads bleed, Mom. Coupla stitches and I'll be fine." I looked at Frank. "Where's Anne?"

"I hope she burned to death in her own fire."

"Marcie, please."

"She tried to kill our daughter."

"I'm well aware of that, but you're not helping."

My parents continued to argue, but I wasn't listening. Something was nagging at me. I felt like there was something I needed to tell them, but I couldn't remember what it was. Frank's sooty forehead creased with worry. I reached out to him, straining with the effort to lift my arm. Then it came to me. "Alex." My voice sounded raspy from the effects of the smoke.

"What is it, Cara?"

I swallowed to moisten my throat and tried again. "She was with Alex. She said her blood was on his coat."

"Alex is in jail, Cara." Frank put his hands on my shoulders, pulling away when I yelped.

"No, he was here with her. I heard them talking."

"Alex couldn't have been here, Kit," said Dad. "Dan wouldn't be here if Alex had broken out of jail." He gestured to where the volunteer firemen were emptying the last of the contents of the tank onto the fire and I saw Dan among them.

I felt a weight go off my chest. "Then who was she talking to?"

***

Gabby Lighthorse finished taping my arm and I sat back in my chair, glad she was done. I hoped for Mel's sake she was gentler with new moms than she was with old quarterbacks. I thanked her anyway, but she shook her head. "That's not going to heal right without a doctor."

"Don't start, Gabby." Clem Solokov had pushed his way through the crowd that had drifted from the fire to Mel's once the water in the tank ran out. Gabby had pronounced my collar bone broken and told my mother not to let me sleep in case I had a concussion, but otherwise I was peachy.

"Don't you tell me what to think, Clem," said Gabby, wagging her finger at him. "I'm tired of patchin' people up around here. You better be talkin' to that lady doctor and I mean today, mister!" She pushed the mayor aside and flounced out, if a sixty-three year old, two hundred and thirty pound woman can be said to flounce. Donny, who'd been dispatched to fetch her, shrugged and hurried out after his grandmother.

"Robert, you're going to have to take Caribou to Juneau as soon as she's strong enough to go."

"Mom by then my bone will have already set. I'm not letting them re-break it just so it'll heal prettier."

"Marcie, leave her alone. She's a grown woman."

Mel and I stared at Dad. Neither of us had ever heard him snap at her before. It was refreshing and a bit scary, all at the same time. My mother opened her mouth, then closed it again, then she turned on Solokov. "This wouldn't be happening if you'd have listened to me."

"I tried, Marcie."

"You obviously didn't try hard enough." They went around the dining area, Clem falling back and my mother advancing, in some kind of bizarre political dance.

"You think she'll win?" Mel whispered to me.

"It wasn't Clem's fault Olivia backed out. What do you suppose is taking Dan so long? How hard can it be to track Anne down?"

"I'm sure he's doing his best, Cara."

"I'll feel a whole lot better when she's in that cell with Alex. Not to mention whoever it is she was talking to. I still want to know how her blood got on Alex's coat and how his coat ended up in the attic."

Dan walked in as I said that, his clothes stained with smoke and ash, his face blackened from fighting the fire. Mel got up and went to get him a cup of coffee. He dropped into the chair across from me. "Fire's out."

"I thought you went after Anne."

"What? Why?" Mel put his coffee on the table in front of him. "What's she done now?"

"She only tried to kill my sister."

There was a rumble behind us and Frank came in. He had a tight hold on a very angry Anne Buchanan. "Take your hands off me!" She saw Dan. "Officer, I want this man arrested."

Dan sighed and got up. "What's the problem?" He pulled out a chair for Anne, who tugged her arm free from Frank and sat like a queen on a throne.

"This man," she pointed at Frank, "kidnapped me at the marina and dragged me in here."

"Why would he do that?"

"How should I know what goes on in the mind of a criminal?"

"Oh, I don't know, Anne," I said. "I think you'd have a pretty good idea."

Her body had stiffened at the sound of my voice and she twisted in her chair to look at me. The color drained from her face. "You were trespassing. I have a right to defend my own property."

"By locking me in a closet and setting the house on fire?"

Her face twitched. "I didn't set any fire. The house is a tinderbox. You told me yourself the whole place needed re-wiring. I'm sure that's what caused the fire."

"Along with a can of gasoline."

Her mouth started working before her answer came. "I don't know what you're talking about."

"That's a lie!"

"I'll show her what we do with murderers around here!" My mom threw herself at Anne, who shrieked and tried to get away from her. Frank shoved Anne back in her chair while my father grabbed onto my mother's waist, slowing her progress.

"Simmer down, both of you!" shouted Dan. Mom glared at him and came to stand beside me, my father trailing after her. Dan threw his hands up, addressing the crowd in the dining area. "Haven't you people got something better to do?"

"Not really," came a familiar voice.

Dan rubbed his forehead. "For God's sake, Earl, go home."

"Anne, who were you talking to at the house today?" I asked, drawing a scowl from Dan.

"Are you insane? I was talking to you, of course."

"After you locked me in the closet."

"I did no such thing."

"Right after you slammed a vase over my head and kicked a chair out from under me."

"You had no right poking your nose into my attic."

"It isn't your house, you lunatic."

"Mom, I've got this."

"No," said Dan staring pointedly first at Mom, then at me. "I've got this. Anne, what were you doing at the house?"

"What was I doing there? What was she doing there?" She pointed at me.

"You're not making it easier for yourself by refusing to answer my questions."

"Wait a minute, Dan." Mayor Solokov stepped out of the crowd, being careful to keep a table between himself and my mother. "Shouldn't you read her rights to her before you ask questions?"

"I haven't arrested her, Clem."

"You should arrest her," I said. "She tried to kill me."

"I did not!"

"Who were you were talking to before you started the fire?"

"Cara, I can handle this."

"I'm just trying to help."

"I want my lawyer." She clamped her mouth shut and crossed her arms in front of her.

"Are you happy now, Clemson?" asked my mother. "You and your stupid Miranda warning."

"You want any charges to stick, don't you, Marcie?" countered the mayor. "Take her up to Juneau with Alex, Dan. Let the state sort it out."

"I can't take her to Lemon Creek for a misdemeanor battery charge."

"Misdemeanor? She hits me with a vase and sets fire to the house with me locked in a closet and you call that a misdemeanor?"

"I never set any fire!"

"I can't charge her with the fire, Cara. I don't have any proof."

"But I heard her, Dan. She was talking to somebody, telling whoever it was she had to act before I found Alex's coat because her blood was on it and the next thing I know, she's pouring gasoline all over the place. If it weren't for Frank, I wouldn't have gotten out alive."

"I don't care what you say," said Anne, but a little of the fervor had gone out of her. "I didn't start that fire."

"Then who did?" asked Dan. She dropped her eyes to the floor and didn't answer. "Come on, Anne. You're going to prison for arson and attempted murder. Is he worth it?"

I pulled a chair over and sat down in front of the older woman. "Anne, you're only hurting yourself. With what I heard, knowing your brother was in jail at the time, they'll drop the charges against Alex." She looked up at me, but still didn't speak. "Whoever you were talking to is probably laughing behind your back right now. You'll be in prison and both of them will be running around free."

Her eyes never left mine and I could almost see the wheels turning as she thought about what I'd said. There was an absolute hush in the room as the whole town, it seemed, waited for her to answer.

"Don't answer that." Mayor Solokov broke into the silence, earning cat-calls from the back of the room. "I'm sorry, people, but once she says she wants a lawyer, questioning has to stop or we can't use what she says."

"A day's training at magistrate school doesn't make you an expert in the law, Clemson."

"Marcie, I'm only trying to do what's right."

"Fine, fine, we'll do it by the book." Dan hauled Anne out of her chair and turned her around, pulling her arms behind her. "Anne Buchanan, you're under arrest. You have the right to remain silent." The townsfolk in the room picked up and finished the warning for him and Dan shook his head at them. "You people watch too much TV."

She struggled. "Wait, wait. You're making a mistake. I didn't set the fire."

Dan looked at the mayor and Solokov looked at Anne. "If you choose to make a statement, you have to waive your right to have an attorney present. Dan, do we have any of those forms over at City Hall?"

"Heck no. I guess I could download one."

"Can't she just tell us?" I asked. "I want to hear what she has to say."

Clem frowned. "Are you sure you want to speak with us without your attorney present?"

"Yes, just take these off."

"You realize that anything you say can and will be used against you in a court of law?"

"For heaven's sake, Clem, I just told her that."

"Fine," he signaled to Dan, who unlocked the handcuffs and hung them back on a loop of his belt. "Talk."

Anne massaged her wrists and pulled herself to her full height. "I defended myself against a trespasser, but I did not set that fire."

"So you keep saying," said Clem. "If you have nothing more to add—"

Dan reached for her arm again but she pulled away. "It was Milo."

I slumped back in my chair, disappointed. "Who's that?"

"Milo Dickerson."

"The developer?" asked Dan.

"You know him?"

"We know of him. Go on. This Milo was in the house with you this morning?"

"Yes and he must have set the fire."

"Start at the beginning." I said. "Alex said you met Dickerson at some kind of event?"

She hesitated. "Tell the truth, Anne," warned Dan.

She ignored him, addressing her remarks to me. "We met at a fundraiser. He's quite successful."

"And he wanted to buy the house."

"When you called about the furnace, I thought it was time we sell for whatever we could get. Milo suggested he buy it and flip it."

"What about Agatha?"

"Aggie hated that house. She wouldn't care if we sold it."

"Why send Alex up to show Dickerson the house?"

"Milo insisted he needed to see the house before he could sell his investment partner on the deal. I wasn't able to get away, so I told Alex I'd split the proceeds with him if he'd convince Milo to buy."

She sat looking expectantly at me, but I wasn't sure what to say. Was she lying or was Alex when he told me she'd followed them up? I looked at Dan.

He picked up the questioning. "Let's cut to the chase. Which one of you killed Mrs. Nash?"

"That's a little blunt, don't you think, Dan?" asked Clem, stepping out of the crowd that frankly, I'd forgotten was there.

"Are you telling me how to do my job?" Dan took a menacing step toward the mayor.

"Well maybe somebody ought to."

"If you knew how to do your job, Clemson, we'd have a doctor in this town."

"That is not my fault."

"Take it outside!" Mom and Clem glared at Dan, but both subsided and he turned his attention back to Anne. "Who killed Mrs. Nash?"

"Don't believe a word she says," came a shout from the door. The voice was familiar, but I couldn't place it. A man walked in, shaking his arm free from the fisherman-turned-police-guard who trailed behind him. He looked to be in his forties, was wearing a pale yellow slicker that would have been more at home in the Caribbean than southern Alaska. He was painfully thin, with the pock-marked complexion of a meth addict.

"Caught him trying to make a break for it, Dan. Just where you thought he'd be."

I looked at Dan, impressed, but his eyes were fixed on the newcomer. "He have the gas can?"

"Three of them. Left them in the boat. Nate's keeping an eye on it."

"Good work. Lab boys are on their way."

"Wow, gas cans in a boat," the man was annoyingly smug. "Hope that's not all the evidence you've got, Pops, cuz I'm going sue the crap out of this town for false arrest."

I finally put a name with the voice. "Milo Dickerson."

He looked at me, his face puzzled at first, then his features hardened. "Caribou King. You're a lot sexier on the phone."

Frank slapped him on the back of the head. "Shut your mouth."

"You're the big real estate developer?" asked my mother. "You couldn't develop a pup tent."

"What's it to you? I got connections."

"You didn't meet him at any society fundraiser, Anne," I said, eying Milo as Frank pushed him into a chair facing the older woman.

"That what she told you?" He snorted. "That's rich."

"Shut up, Milo," Anne snapped at him, but he ignored her.

"My old man was dumb enough to marry her. I didn't even know about it. I met this old bag at his funeral. He cut me outta his will for her, how's that for charity event?"

"Is that true, Anne?"

"He wouldn't know the truth if it bit him. His father disowned him years ago. I had nothing to do with it."

"Ain't that the pot calling the kettle black?" Milo smiled at Anne's obvious discomfort.

"How drunk was Alex," I asked my mother, "to have believed this guy was a real estate developer?"

"Shut your mouth, slut," said Milo, earning another slap on the back of the head from Frank only this one must have been hard enough to make him see stars. "Watch yourself, or I'll sue you for police brutality."

"I ain't the police," said Frank.

"Enough," said Dan. He looked up at the fisherman, who looked to be enjoying the show. "Get Alex, will ya?" We all waited in strained silence until he reappeared, pushing Alex along in front of him. He looked confused to see Milo, but he accepted the chair Dan offered without a word. "I don't want to hear anything from you three but the truth." Anne stared at her hands, Alex looked at Milo and Milo was picking dirt from under his fingernails. "Okay, you know what I think happened to Mrs. Nash? I think Alex and Milo rented a boat and came up here to see the house. Anne followed you to Alaska."

"I wasn't here."

"Give it a rest," said Milo.

"I've already confirmed the flight into Juneau, Anne. Only you didn't go straight to Coho Bay, did you?"

A flush started to spread across Anne's face. "I took the ferry."

"After you pulled a copy of the title to the house."

"You knew?" Alex twisted around in his chair. "You knew and you never told me? Not even after you knew she was dead?"

"I didn't think it mattered."

"How could it not matter? How could you lie to me like that, Anne?"

"She's been lying about a lot of things, Alex," said Dan. "On the day she was killed, Mrs. Nash told you she owned the house. Milo went out and knocked on doors, trying to find anyone else dumb enough to sell for pennies on the dollar—"

"Pennies on the dollar?" interrupted Anne.

"He offered you fifty thousand dollars, right?" I asked and she nodded. "The land alone is worth at least a quarter of a million."

"What?" Her mouth dropped open for a minute, then she jumped up and grabbed Milo by his yellow slicker. His chair tipped over backwards as she shook him like a rag doll. "You son of a—"

"Sit down!" It took Dan and Frank both to pull Anne off her stepson. She cursed and kicked and threatened all three of them with more strength than I'd thought possible for a woman her age.

Close to thirty minutes went by before order was restored. Dan moved the three of them further apart and stationed two men behind each one. Anne sat in her chair, rocking back and forth. Milo looked shaken and Alex kept looking back and forth between the two of them.

Since none of them were volunteering information, Dan went on with his narrative. "Alex argued with Mrs. Nash then went to find Anne, but you weren't where you told him you'd be, were you?"

"I don't know what you mean."

"You were watching from the trailhead. You saw them leave, then you went after Mrs. Nash." Anne didn't answer. She just kept rocking, staring at the floor. "She'd bought a gun to protect herself from bears. That was the gun that killed her. How did you get your hands on it?"

"I didn't kill her!" wailed Anne. "I didn't."

"Alex left his coat at the house," I said, keeping my voice soft as though I were speaking to a frightened child. She didn't look at me, but she stopped rocking. "How did your blood get on his coat?"

Anne held out her hand, shaking so badly, I had to take hold of it to see what she was showing me. A slash cut across her palm, nearly healed. "She threatened me. She picked up a knife and told me to get out of her house. Her house! That ... woman ... killed my mother. She tried to kill me! I grabbed the knife and it cut my hand."

"So you used the coat to stop the bleeding?" asked Dan. "Why didn't you take it with you when you left?"

"I went into the bathroom," said Anne, her words coming in gasps between sobs. "To wash off the blood."

Alex scooted his chair over to her and put an arm on her back. "It's all right, Anne. You didn't do anything wrong."

Anne stared at her brother, who was looking at her with wide eyes. Tears welled in her eyes and streamed down her cheeks as she spoke. "She laughed at me, Alex. She had the gall to call me a disappointment to father. That whore called me a disappointment. She destroyed our family. She murdered our mother."

"What are you talking about?" demanded my mother.

"She and that good for nothing husband of hers told father to put mother out of her misery. Can you imagine? Like she was some sort of dog you ask the vet to put down." Sobs shook her body, choking off her story. Milo stared up at the ceiling, looking for all the world like a bored teenager. Alex put an arm around his sister's shoulders and slowly she regained control.

"She deserved what she got."

"Anne," Alex started, but he didn't finish. He drew his arm away from her.

"I couldn't help it," Anne's voice rose, though I wasn't sure whether she was trying to convince Alex or herself. "I saw the gun. Who keeps a gun in the bathroom? I thought it was a gift from God. I was looking for something to wrap up my hand and I found the gun. I didn't think about it, I just did it. Then I panicked. I heard someone coming and I hid in the bedroom."

"You were there?" said Alex. "You saw me pick up the gun? Why didn't you say something?"

"I didn't know it was you," said Anne. "I heard someone come in and then run out. I assumed some neighbor had heard the shot and was going for help."

"But you let the police think it was me," said Alex.

"I wouldn't have let them convict you. I would have thought of something," said Anne.

"Telling the truth would have been good," said Dan.

"What about the coat?" I asked. "Alex said it was beside Mrs. Nash. He went to pick it up and that's how he ended up picking up the gun."

"I must have dropped them both there," said Anne. She grabbed Alex by the arm. "I'm so sorry. I wouldn't have let you go to jail. I tried to protect you. I hid the coat in the attic."

"That's what I found!" I said. "But why hide the coat? Why not just take it with you? If you thought it was a neighbor who came in, then you had no way of knowing it was Alex who'd picked up the gun. Take the coat and there's nothing to tie you two to the murder."

"Oh for crying out loud," said Milo. "She knew it was Alex. She watched him from the bathroom. She saw him pick up the gun and decided to frame him. She put the coat in the attic thinking the cops would find it. Didn't occur to her until later that her blood was on the coat too. Idiot."

"Shut up!" Anne screamed. She made a leap for him, but the two men Dan had stationed behind her pulled her back into her chair. She turned to her brother. "I swear, I never meant for them to think you shot her. I assumed they'd think it was a suicide."

Alex moved his chair away from hers. "That's why we had to come back. You never cared about what the police knew. You just wanted to get that coat to save your own skin."

"Why didn't you take the coat, Anne?" I asked.

"Because I couldn't." She spat out the words. "You and that black woman were at the house. I waited for you to come out, but you were taking forever. I had to run when I heard the ferry."

"Why would you need to take the ferry?" asked Alex. "We had a boat."

Anne's mouth opened, but no sound came out. Milo again filled the void. "She never cared about you, dude. She got you drunk on the boat and then pointed you at the old bag's funeral."

"Why would you do that, Anne?" Alex sounded like a wounded child, questioning a parent.

"To keep all the focus on you, dude," said Milo. "She got me to call the old bag's lawyer asking about the house."

"You did that on your own, you fool. You were the one who thought she wouldn't have an heir and they'd sell the house cheap."

Milo shrugged. "Say what you want. I know what happened."

"Why did you knock Cara off her chair and lock her in the closet?" asked Dan.

Anne rolled her eyes. "She fell off the chair. You locked me out of the bedroom."

"Because you tried to kill me!"

She dismissed my accusation with a wave of her hand. "I heard the crash. By the time I got in, you were flat out on the floor."

"Why lock me in if you weren't trying to kill me?"

"Because Milo was there."

"Hey, I didn't know there was anybody in the house when this old bat told me to torch it."

"I never told you any such thing."

"What was Alex's role in all of this?" Dan asked.

Milo shrugged and sat back in his chair. Alex looked intensely at Anne. "Tell them," he implored, but she didn't respond. "I didn't have anything to do with Mrs. Nash's death and you all know," he turned to the townsfolk, who had been watching the back and forth between the three in stunned silence, "I was in jail when the fire happened."

"I think we've heard enough, Dan," said Clem. "Let the boys in Juneau sort it out."

Chapter 13

Three days before Christmas, I went to meet the ferry. My arm was still in the sling because it was simpler to leave it there than have the same argument with my mother every morning. I hate anything that restricts movement but I had to admit, it hurt less in the sling than out. It was snowing so I'd had Mel toss my heavy coat over my shoulders and button what she could. I'd lost my favorite coat in the fire so I was stuck with this one until I could get to Juneau to shop. Shipping costs to Alaska made shopping on line unappealing and since anything I ordered would have to be delivered by Kenny anyway, I usually just rode up with him whenever I needed anything.

I paced the pier impatiently, waiting for the lumbering ferry to dock. As soon as the gangplank extended, a slender figure ran down it and threw her arms around me. I gasped in pain, but I did my best to hug her back. "Olivia! I'm so thrilled you could make it for Christmas. I was afraid you wouldn't be able to get away."

She grinned, the stress and sadness she'd worn on her last trip to Coho Bay replaced by a dimple in her cheek and a bounce in her step. When she spoke, her words were quick and her tone animated. "I've worked every holiday since I started med school. When I heard what happened to you, I marched in there and told them I was going home for Christmas and here I am!"

Her delight was infectious and I threw the only arm I could move around her. "Don't call Coho Bay home in front of Mom unless you're ready to back it up."

"Ranting about your collar bone, I take it?"

"You'd think I never broke a bone before. Can you believe she wants me to go to the hospital?"

Olivia accepted her suitcase, a small carry-on bag, from the luggage minder and took hold of my good arm. "I can see it still hurts. How long has it been, three weeks?"

"Pretty close."

"Well, I'll take a look when we get home, and I do mean home. I haven't been able to stop thinking about Coho Bay since I left. When you're mom called, I made up my mind then and there that this was where I was meant to be."

"Hopefully not just because I'm a klutz."

"Marcie said somebody hit you and pushed you off a chair."

"I can't prove she pushed me."

"Insane. I hope they're in jail."

"Anne pled guilty on the assault charge but she's fighting the arson. Her son's keeping his mouth shut but Dan thinks they have enough to make the murder charge stick."

"That what Gram's attorney told me. What a horrible way for her to die and for nothing. Absolutely nothing."

"I know. Makes me sick. Poor Doc's gotta be rolling over in his grave and now you've lost the house on top of everything else."

"You're safe, that's all that matters. You told me yourself it would probably be better to tear down the house and start over than try to fix it."

"So you're going to build?"

She smiled but shook her head. "You'll have to wait and see."

There were hugs all around when we got to Mel's apartment. Olivia took me into the bedroom so she could take a good look at my shoulder. After some painful pokes and prodding, she stood back and frowned.

"Tell her to go to the hospital."

"Mom, cut it out. I'm fine. Aren't I, Olivia?"

"Then what is that huge bump on your collar bone?"

"That's called a callus," Olivia answered. "When a break heals, it forms a callus as sort of a bridge to knit the two pieces together. Her body will absorb most of it in time and the lump will become less pronounced."

"I told you I was fine."

"But you don't look happy, Olivia," Mel observed. "Is something wrong?"

"I'd need an x-ray to be sure but the break appears displaced. Had I been here when it happened, I could have re-set it, though we've been seeing better long-term results with surgery even then. Now it would require surgery to set it."

"I'm not having surgery."

"Caribou, if that is what Olivia recommends, that is what you're going to do."

"I'm a grown woman and I can make my own decisions. Olivia, is this something I have to do?"

"It'll heal the way it is," she answered. "It'll be slower and it won't be pretty, but it'll be functional. If it were me, I'd have the surgery."

"Functional is good enough for me. Now, can we all please stop talking about my shoulder?"

"No promises," said Mel, sticking her tongue out at me and ducking out of the room before I could retaliate. I put my shirt and sling back on and followed Mom and Olivia into the family room. They had their heads together, whispering like schoolgirls. I tried to get close enough to hear, but Mom shooed me away.

The family room was decorated for Christmas, with a living fir tree on a table under the window that faced the road. Mel had decorated it with home-made ornaments since we'd left our collection at the cottages. With a string of popcorn and tiny baby gifts hung on the branches it looked charming. There were a few gifts under the tree but in my family, Christmas was less about the presents than it was being together. I had a hunch we might see piles of gifts as Mel and Bent brought more grandchildren into the fold.

Dad was settled on one of two rocking chairs on one side of the fire, with Bent and Mel on a loveseat on the other. Dan was sitting on one side of a couch that faced the fire and Frank was on the other. Both of them started to stand when I came into the room, but my mother waved her hand. "Sit, sit." I made a beeline for the second rocker, but she squelched me. "Caribou, don't take my chair."

Both men were watching me expectantly from the couch. "Olivia?" I asked, hoping for an assist.

"No thank you." Her mouth turned up at the corners. "I'm good." Mom was dragging an ottoman over for her to sit on.

I smiled weakly at the two men, who each held out a hand to me. I took Dan's, disappointing Frank, but my bad arm was in a sling and Dan was on my good side. I sat uncomfortably between them. "So what's all the whispering, Mom?"

She cleared her throat and sat ram-rod straight in her chair, which is tough to do in a rocker but she managed it. "Olivia has agreed to live and practice medicine in Coho Bay as soon as she finishes her residency."

"That's great!" I would have jumped up if I weren't penned in, but she wasn't lacking welcome.

"Thank you, everybody. I know this is gonna sound strange, with the circumstances, but I felt at home here as soon as I stepped off the boat when Cara and Dan brought me here. It's so beautiful and everyone has been so friendly." Her voice caught. "I know Gram would have been glad."

"We're glad too," said my mother, "and not only because this town needs a doctor."

"Sure, Mother." Mel rolled her eyes.

"I wouldn't be happy having someone I didn't like and respect move here, no matter how great the need. Olivia is a lovely young woman and she'll make an excellent addition to our community."

"I agree," said Frank. A look passed between him and Olivia that made me catch my breath. It vanished so quickly I wondered if I'd been mistaken.

"We can draw up plans for your new home before you leave," I said, forcing my mind out of dangerous territory. "We can't start building until the snow melts and, of course, we're all crazy busy here as soon as the season opens but we'll figure out a place for you to stay."

"Actually, Caribou, the plans are already drawn but the house we'll be building will be ours."

"Yours, Mother?" The color had drained from Mel's face.

"Marcie, don't tease the girl," said Dad.

"Your parents are trading my property for theirs," said Olivia, reaching over to give Mel's knee a reassuring squeeze.

"You're going to build a house next door to Mel?" I asked.

"No, silly." Olivia laughed. "I'm going to take over their log cabin. You know how much I loved that place. Marcie and Bob offered me the trade if I didn't mind living so far out of town."

"I'm afraid this is coming as a big shock to you girls, but Melody, you haven't used your cabin since you married Bentley."

"I've got no problem with it," agreed Mel.

"Caribou, you've been talking about staying in town year-round so we thought you might not mind the arrangement."

"Mom, it's your property, yours and Dads. The gallery is all I need."

"Of course." She looked at Frank. "This means we will not have a place for you to rent next winter, Franklin."

"That's not so bad," he said. "I was feeling bad about letting Jack down so I went out there to talk to him. He convinced me to give the mill another try. He's got a dry cabin out there that nobody's lived in for years."

"I remember that cabin," I said. "Johnny and I used to go there and tell ghost stories. It's creepy."

Frank laughed. "It is a little creepy, but it's a roof over my head."

"You can't live in a dry cabin, Frank," said Olivia. "Why don't you take one of the girl's cabins? I'm hoping to rent the other out. I've got student loans to pay." Again, the look between them was brief but electric.

"Then it's settled," said my mother. "In the spring we'll break ground. We'll stay here until it's ready, of course, but at least you'll have free babysitting."

"Now, that I can live with," said Bent. "And on that note, let's eat!"

Frank jumped up and offered his hand to Olivia, who blushed as she reached up to accept. The two of them went down to the kitchen without so much as a backward glance. Bent helped Mel up and they walked arm in arm toward the stairs, but Dan and I just sat, staring at the fire. "You upset about the cabin, Cara?" asked Dan when I didn't speak.

"What? Oh, yes, I guess I am a bit. I loved that cabin, but it was kind of a pain to be in the middle of nowhere all winter and I do love my apartment."

We didn't talk for a few minutes, then Dan spoke again. "Look, I know I'm not the type to run into burning buildings."

"Stop it. I'm sure if you'd been there, you would have done the same thing."

"Still, a girl's gotta love a guy who saves her life."

"Is this your way of asking if I'm more interested in Frank than I am in you? If you didn't notice, he just walked off with another woman."

"He's rattling your chain because you took my hand instead of his."

"You think so?" I felt a pang of guilt at the hurt look in Dan's eyes. "It doesn't matter. You're a nice man and I like you very much, Dan."

He made a motion like he was stabbing a dagger into his chest. "Ouch. The nice guy line. Next you'll tell me you just want to be friends."

I smiled, considering. I liked Dan, but there was none of the pulse-pounding excitement with him that I felt whenever Frank shot me one of his smoldering looks. He was the man that took my breath away, but that didn't mean he was the man I should trust my heart to. Dan was sweet and steady and while that kind of guy didn't grace the covers of romance books, he'd be someone I could always count on. Like a brother.

"I don't know what to say Dan. I like you too much to lead you on, but I don't know if that will ever take us anywhere."

He picked up my hand and waited until I raised my eyes. "Any man who walks away because you aren't ready to make a commitment isn't a man worth being with anyway." My heart gave a lurch and I held my breath as he leaned forward to kiss me.

"Cara? Dan? Pull yourselves apart and get down here. I got a hungry baby on board." Mel's voice floated up the stairs and I heard her laughter retreating back into the kitchen.

Moment broken, I leaned my head against Dan's chin. "Rain check?" I asked.

"Absolutely."

THE END

ABOUT THE AUTHOR

 Linda Crowder is best known for her *Jake and Emma Mystery* series, set in her adopted home town of Casper, Wyoming. The series features a pair of accidental detectives who join forces with the local police to track down killers. Her books are a delightful blend of mystery, relationships, humor and tears. Linda and her husband fell in love with Alaska on their first trip there in 2014. Her love of the Alaskan Inside Passage led her to place the *Caribou King Mystery* series in the mythical cruise ship town of Coho Bay, Alaska.

From the Author

Thank you for reading my book about the people in Coho Bay, Alaska. The Inside Passage is one of the most beautiful places on earth and it's my pleasure to bring it into your home. I was there last in May 2016 and saw whales, seals, sea lions and more eagles than I could count. The people are some of the most friendly I've met and I appreciate all of them who took the time to answer my questions about what it's like to live in this northern paradise.

If you enjoyed *The Deadly Art of Love and Murder*, I would appreciate if you posted a quick review our favorite book website. If you visit my website, http://www.lindajcrowder.com/ sign up for my newsletter. Also, please read the first book in the Caribou King mystery series *The Deadly Art of Deception*.

Can't wait? You might enjoy my other series, *Jake and Emma Mysteries*. Jake and Emma Rand are a couple of accidental detectives who are forced into catching killers when they find the body of a woman on their fence line in Casper, Wyoming. To meet Jake and Emma, look for *Too Cute to Kill* at your favorite book seller.

Other books by Linda Crowder

Jake and Emma Mysteries:

Too Cute to Kill
Main Street Murder
Justice for Katie
Death Changes Everything
Coming soon: *A Body on the Ballot*